# ARMORDILLO

## MICHAEL POLILLO

# Contents

## CHAPTER 1

The meteor wasn't invited, but it arrived all the same. It was a clear night in Clapham, Texas. One of those nights that Karl loved to sit outside and watch the stars. He sat on the porch of his three story farmhouse and stared into the dark sky. He and his sister and brother, Judy and Bill, live together and used their land as one of the biggest insect farms in the country. Insects are a booming food resource in America and they figured they jump in when the water was still cold. Their insect of choice is the house cricket. They imported several thousand from Thailand to start their business. And business was good. The family didn't even mind the incessant chirping as it was a reminder of their success. Most people in Clapham worked with insects. If they weren't farming them, they were studying them. Insects may be the food of the future and scientists want to be on the ground floor to make sure they're safe for people to eat.

The shooting star didn't escape Karl's gaze. It dropped right into the woods that surrounded their farmhouse. He scrambled off his porch to wake up his brother and sister. It wasn't the first time Karl had ruined their sleep. Karl didn't heed their countless warnings. Sure it was never anything of value before when he had woken them up. *But what if tonight's the night when it's gold?* Judy and Bill didn't seem the point in striking it rich when they were already well off, but they entertained Karl anyway. The three siblings went off into the night trying to find the fallen pot of gold.

"You know it's probably just another collection of shit from a plane," said Bill.

"If it is then we can use it as fertilizer," said Karl.

"He's joking right?" said Bill to Judy.

Judy shrugged and followed her brothers through the woods. It was a warm August night and the trees welcomed the family within them. A series of broken branches led them to a clearing in the woods. A large crater swallowed up trees and decimated a chunk of the Earth. *How could a little meteor do this?*

"Where is it?" said Bill.

"It probably burnt up in the atmosphere," said Judy.

"If it burnt up in the atmosphere I wouldn't had seen it, stupid," said Karl.

"It burning it in the atmosphere is the only reason you saw it," said Judy.

"Then explain this crater," said Karl.

"It could be a sinkhole for all we know," said Judy.

"I think I'd know if there were a sinkhole here," said Karl.

"It looks pretty deep to me," said Bill.

"It probably is, especially if its a sinkhole," said Judy.

Clouds formed in the sky taking away the moon. It became hard for them to see their hands at their sides without the moon's guiding light.

"We've got to get down in there and find it," said Karl.

"Maybe it did land, but I can't see shit now. We should get back to the farm and check it out tomorrow before we fall in and get hurt," said Judy.

"And let that damn astronomer take for herself? She thinks because it's science she doesn't need to obey private property signs," said Karl.

"We don't have any private property signs," said Bill.

"I guess we should be getting some then so that bitch stops coming round here without our permission," said Karl.

"Karl, I don't think we're even on our property anymore," said Judy.

"Come on Karl, it's late. If we come back at sunrise we'll be here before anyone could have the chance to."

"If you two want to go back that's fine, but I'm staying and seeing if we struck gold. It's finders, keepers and it's ours for the taking," said Karl.

The ground beneath them began to stir. Their legs shifted beyond their own control and they fell to their asses. They realized someone or rather something else had beaten them to their prize.

A huge shadowy blob with spikes at the top scurried under them. They could see it moving around in the pit like a dog trying to escape a bath session. An acrid smell of rotten eggs carried to the family's nostrils. They pinched their noses and squinted their eyes nearly about to burst with tears.

"I can barely breathe," said Karl.

"What the hell is it?" said Bill.

"Whatever it is, I ain't sticking around to see if it's friendly," said Judy.

"What if its the meteor? It could be some sort of alien?" said Karl.

Judy already quit the conversation and took off into the woods leaving Bill and Karl behind her.

"Damn it Judy, get back here," said Bill.

"Let her go, but she's not getting any of the money," said Karl.

The shadow began to rise as Karl and Bill stared frozen in awe. It seemed whatever it was had gone from a crouching position into a standing one. It easily stood towered over the brothers and cleared some of the tree line.

"Jesus, it's huge," said Bill again.

Bill took a few steps closer. The shadow shifted and spritzing sound came from its now apparent clawed hands. A shower of black goo covered Bill's legs. He tried to move, but was stuck in place. A scream escaped his lungs before the rest of him was completely covered. He slumped to the ground engulfed by the tar like substance.

"Bill! Hold on, I'll help you, I'm going to kill this son of a bitch," said Karl.

Karl ran to a tree and broke off a rotten branch. He tossed it at the shadow with a thud and it fell to the ground into pieces. The shadow didn't react. Karl went back and found a heavy rock to hurl at the creature. It clanged off and this time the beast stirred. It didn't seem hurt, but it did notice. The shadow shifted towards the farmer.

A claw went straight through Karl's chest. His mouth became a faucet of blood as he was lifted into the air. He looked down to see his brother covered in tar and diminishing in the darkness. His eyes widened as he saw what had impaled him. It was a plated face with two eyes and a large snout. It's mouth opened and Karl's head was engulfed with a horrifying warmth. The last sounds he heard before the crunch was that of his cricket farm.

Judy's feet ran double time back towards the farm. She could hear the screams of her brothers behind her. She'd have to get some backup if she was going to save them. Those sounds of the crickets guided her. They were sirens in the dark calling her to safety.

The large shadow moved silently in the night. It came upon the farm and within minutes all the chirping was gone. There wasn't a cricket left unharmed. Those not sprayed with black goo were eaten and those swallowed whole wish they were sprayed.

Judy made it back to their farmhouse. She stopped in the clearing outside the woods and held her hand up to her ear to hear. There was nothing. No sound at all.

*If I could just get to the truck. I can get out, I can get help.*

A few seconds later and her eyes were set on her salvation. The green 1996 Ford Pickup was there grazing where it always was. Entirely dependable even twenty years since it was made. She climbed inside and searched her pockets for the keys. *Where the fuck are they? Did Karl ever give them back this afternoon?*

*That stupid fuck never puts them back where they're supposed to go. How many times have I told him to keep them on the seat?*

Judy rummaged through the truck. Nothing in the glove compartment. Nothing in the center console. Nothing in the pouch behind the backseat. Luckily the double barrel was still laying in the backseat. Judy felt some blood trickling down from her head. She pulled down the sun visor to take a look at the damage. Down plopped the keys into her lap. Her cut wasn't bad either. *Of course they'd be there. He probably put them there thinking we'd look there first. Why wouldn't we check the sun visor at night?*

The truck started with a kick of the engine and it zipped down the driveway. Judy let out the largest sigh of relief she ever had and wiped her brow in victory. Whatever the fuck that was seemed gone and she was getting further away. There was plenty of gas in the tank and Jim's bar was a swift ten minutes from their farm. She could get help there. One of the local truckers or even the scientist Karl hates would be there. Anyone would be nice to see right now.

A shadow lay in the middle of the road. Judy slowed down the truck to take a look. It was some sort of animal. It was covered completely in what looked like black tar. It's as if it this poor soul was dipped in a pool of ink and left to dry on the warm night's asphalt. She reached for the shotgun and held it in her hands still sitting in the driver's seat. Judy flicked on the high beams and the figure became human, but even more, it became Bill. There was no mistaken those coveralls he wears even if they were completely black. *What the fuck?* He was army crawling on his belly across the road. Judy froze in fear inside the truck. She wanted to get out there and carry her brother in. Her body said otherwise. All she did was watch as her brother extended his arm and forced his body to move with it. Bill cocked his head in the lights of the truck and yelled for help. It was guttural and sounded like his was choking on the word. The cry rang out again. Judy could almost hear her brother's vocal chords snapping with his pleas. Judy herself snapped out of the momentary coma to jump out of the truck. She did run to her brother and bent down to comfort him, shotgun still in hand.

"Bill, it's gonna be alright, just stay calm."

"Judy?"

Bill's voice became a whisper.

"Who else?" said Judy.

"I'm sorry, I can't see anything."

Judy caught a better look at her brother in the headlights of the truck. Bill's eyes looked like they were stuck shut from the tar-like substance he was covered in. He smelled horrific. It was even worse than the time he had been skunked as a child. She dipped her finger into the goo and it was effectively adhesive when brought between her pointer and thumb. It felt tingly and almost as it were burning her skin. She wiped her fingers on her pants.

"Where's Karl?"

"It got him," said Bill.

"He's dead?" said Judy.

"You have to get out of here Judy, you have to get us the fuck out of here."

"Can you stand?"

"No, that fucking thing broke my legs. I can barely move at all."

Judy lifted Bill into her arms and in the closer light saw the truth. Bill's eyes weren't stuck shut. They were gone. The sockets leaked the black tar when she lifted him up showing their emptiness. Judy gulped to fight back her vomit.

"What's wrong?" said Bill.

"Nothing, I'm going to get you out of here."

A growl sung through the air towards the sister and brother. The Earth shook and the creature burst out from the ground near the truck.

A claw came down on the pickup sending it through the air. The sound of metal crunching and glass shattering followed.

Judy stood with Bill in her arms as the creature drew near. It towered over them. Judy could tell this son of a bitch was over thirty feet easy even without a moon shining down.

"I'm going to have to get you to the hospital, or town, or hell even if we can make it to Jim's bar," said Judy.

Bill mumbled what seemed to be an affirmation, but it wasn't clear.

Judy slung Bill over her shoulder and ran into the woods, shotgun in hand. His body was squirming and twitching. Her brother was heavier than she remembered. She hadn't carried him since they were kids. With every step the weight seemed not so bothersome. Judy didn't even notice it anymore after a hundred feet. It was as if she was barely carrying anything at all. Even in these hilly woods it didn't seem so tiresome. The kicking of Bill's feet stopped after a minute too. He seemed to have calmed down.

Although she wasn't tired from carrying her brother, she was tired from running. She needed to catch her breath a moment before continuing their marathon into town.

She plopped her brother onto the ground beside her. The reason why he became so light was quickly apparent. Bill's legs and arms had fallen off during the run. Black ooze leaked from where her brother's limbs once were. Judy screamed into the night at the sight of her brother's limbless lifeless corpse. She took off into the night. She didn't get far as an unlucky root brought her face to the grass.

The earth beneath her quaked and the attacker reemerged out of the ground. Bits of dirt and rock went flying through the air as the creature steadied itself.

The clouds parted allowing the moon to shine down. Judy finally caught a proper glimpse of her assailant. It stood on its hind legs like a gigantic knight with large ears. It had massive razor sharp claws at the end of each hand. Armor covered it head to tail. Huge plates covered its humped back. A long nose protruded from its natural helmet. A massive tail trailed behind the beast. It too was covered in the plating. It let out a thunderous roar bearing its many teeth.

*Alright you son of a bitch, this ends now. You may have killed my brothers, but you won't kill anyone else.*

She brought the shotgun up, aimed it at the creature's head and fired. There was no blast. There was only the sound of the hammer clicking. It was empty.

*Great the one time he actually listens to me about how dangerous it is to keep the gun loaded is the one time I need it loaded.*

Judy dropped the shotgun to her side and stood tall against the beast. She looked to the stars one last time as she took her final breath before she was engulfed by the tar substance spitting out from the creature's wrists. Her corpse slumped down into the fresh crater the creature had made. The beast curled its massive plated body into a ball and jumped into the air like a volleyball being swatted at the beginning of a serve.

The Armordillo had awakened.

CHAPTER 2

The ball shimmered in the sky as it fell. It had just been thrown at 90 mph before hitting a bat that sent it flying through the air. It was a warm afternoon on the field full of teens playing baseball. The ball fell right into the glove of the center fielder. The game was over with that simple catch and the Maryland Trouts had defeated their rival the Brixton Bruisers. The series had been close, but that last catch cinched it for the Trouts. It was all over now.

Jack Strafer watched it all from the stands.  A summer full of kids playing their favorite game, the crowd cheering, and the sun glaring along with it. He wasn't one of the many parents that made up the audience, but instead was the journalist covering the series. It wasn't a bad gig by any means, but it grew old after the hundredth writeup on youth sports. Even this championship game while entertaining wasn't what Jack had signed up for when becoming a writer. He had been following the Maryland Trouts since their first game this season and it was his luck that they went all the way.

Jack stood around 5'10" with jet black hair. His parents were from Rarotonga, an island in the south pacific, but he himself was born in America. Hell he never even left the states to see his parents birthplace. His most distinguishing feature would be his left arm being prosthetic. A mix of plastic and metal was all he had from the elbow down.

Unfortunately Jack had been covering high school sports extensively since he graduated college. It's been three months of angry parents, brat kids, and disgusting food.

Even more unfortunate is that local sports was one of the few reasons why people even continued to buy papers and keep small news companies afloat.

It's worth it for the kids but Jack wanted more. He always enjoyed sports, but was never fond of playing them given his condition. He could appreciate it from afar even if not participating. He wanted to be an investigative journalist. One that really made a difference in society. He wanted to break open cold cases and bring justice to those who deserved it. But he was here instead. His editor had promised he'd eventually get to that point in life in enough time. Jack was growing tired of waiting and each game seemed to drag on longer than the last.

Jack Strafer went over to the dugout for a quote. The proud parents stood by their son and smiled continuously as Jack asked questions. The typical how did it feel to win and what do you plan to do next. The kid gave the appropriate responses of saying it was a team effort achieved through lots of practice and collaboration. It was rare for Jack to get an asshole kid for an interview. He was good at telling when his subject would play ball with his questions or when they'd want to make a fuss. Luckily this kid was one of the normal ones and that made his job all the easier albeit boring. Jack did always put on a good front. He never openly showed his disinterest. He never wanted to discourage the kids from having a good time and enjoying their victory. He especially never wanted to hear complaints about him being sent to his editor.

Jack tightened his arm as he sat on the hood of his car and called his editor, Susan Tombs. She picked up with a cheery voice that Jack never minded hearing. She always seemed in control which was something Jack took comfort in having as a boss. Some would mistake her upbeat attitude for being weak which she was strong enough to play into when it suited her best. It was in complete contrast to Jack's voice. His voice could stop bullets when he would yell and burn hairs when trying to whisper.

"Hey Jack, how'd the game go?"

"Great, it looks like the Trouts are the new champions of the fifteenth division of little league baseball."

"Congrats to them, you'll have the story for me soon?"

"I'll have it for you in a half hour."

"Good and make sure you get a few more pictures before everyone leaves. Parents are breathing down my neck for not having more pictures."

"Not enough pictures? These fuckers are recording everything on their phones the entire game,"

"Hey if more photos get them to buy our papers then we'll give 'em more photos."

"Fine I'll get one of the pitcher."

"Do a whole piece on the pitcher. We could do a small piece every week on every player on the team and have enough covered til football championships."

"Alright I'm going, but I still want to talk to you."

"I'll be here."

Jack went back and snapped a few pictures of the pitcher and the team. He asked how it felt to win the championship and what he wanted to do when he was older.

Most of the kids would answer they wanted to play sports professionally, but his pitcher said he'd like to be an athletic trainer. It was not often for kids to be so honest about their aspirations. Jack wondered about himself at the pitcher's age. He wondered if he knew his life would have ended up the way it has.

He thanked the pitcher and his parents and both teams and the crowd dispersed. Jack was soon the only one left in the parking lot.

Jack hopped into his car and reclined in the driver's seat as he rung back his editor.

"Isn't there anything else I could be writing besides youth sports?" said Jack.

"It's what pays the bills right now Jack."

"I know, but I'd take anything else."

"Anything?"

"You said that as if there's something else I could be covering. What is it?"

"It's something Betty was going to cover, but she's got gastroenteritis."

"What the fuck is gastro- whatever you said?"

"She's leaking both ends, Jack. Don't you know anything?"

"You could just say she's sick."

"She's sick, Jack and she can't go on the assignment she was suppose to cover."

"Sure fine I'll take it."

"You don't even know what it is yet."

"I don't care. I'll take it. It can't be that bad, right?"

"You ever hear of Clapham?"

"Should I have?"

"They're the biggest supplier of insects as food in the nation."

"So you want me to do a piece on edible bugs?"

"Not exactly. A scientist name Rebecca Nove wants to see how the ongoing meteor shower will affect the bug population."

"Why would meteors affect bugs?"

"That's what you're going there to find out."

"Yeah maybe they'll grow to the size of houses and take revenge on us eating them. Speaking of, who would ever want to eat bugs anyway?"

"I wish they'd grow huge. Something like that would put us on the map and you wouldn't have to spend your summer chasing baseball quotes with helicopter parents. But hell, we're all going to be eating bugs soon enough, Jack. There'll be a McCricket sandwich within ten years with the way the world's going. Most countries are already devouring the little fuckers."'

"How many days do you think it'd be?"

"I don't know, three or four?"

"You want me to cover a meteor shower for four nights?"

"What's the matter, Jack? Never heard of the Perseids?"

"No. Has anyone? Who gives a shit about meteors anyway? I'm not sure who would want to read a piece about this."

"You're really going to bash the first thing I give you that isn't high school sports?"

"Fine, I'll do it."

"No one is pressuring you Jack, you're the one complaining about the lack of action. I can let someone else take it if you want to spend the rest of the month interviewing these kids."

"Yeah, but it feels like a downgrade, going from watching sports to watching rocks in the sky."

"You've got some ego for a kid barely out of college. If your head is in the stars you may as well write about them."

"I don't see why I can't do a phone interview after the shower passes."

"Because I don't want you to do an interview over the phone. I want you to get out there in nature and experience the stars, the bugs, and the woods in person. And I want pictures of it all too."

"I already said I'd do it. But you do know that my phone is telling it's a 6 hour drive."

"I thought you said you'd take any gig? That you wanted a chance to prove yourself as a writer."

"So that means I have to pay for my own gas?"

"We all have to make sacrifices Jack. It hasn't been easy for any of us."

"Sacrifices? I'm already using my damn car as an office as it is."

"You know we had to close the offices to help cut down costs. The rent for them is going to paying you now. Not to mention it's keeping the printers running."

"You're at least going to pay me right?"

"Don't be silly, Jack, of course we're paying you the standard rate we agreed upon."

Jack drove a 1972 red Ford Pinto. It was a gift given to him by his father when he first got his license. His dad's reasoning was that if he destroyed it then it didn't matter. He was learning to drive with only one arm after all. Jack proved his father wrong and has continued to drive the out of date car. It didn't bother him much and he knew he'd be driving it for years to come with a journalist's salary.

The pinto was a bit tight, but Jack had removed the back seats for his makeshift office. There were newspapers, clothes, notebooks, and paperback novels scattered throughout the car. He lived more in his car than in his apartment. There was even a stack of papers that contain a novel he's been trying to write for three years. His netbook laid underneath a pillow he'd use when traveling and couldn't afford a motel. That had been often than not recently given him following around the Trouts. He hadn't sleep in a real bed in three weeks. *I guess I can do another three nights.*

"Where and when am I meeting this scientist?"

"You're meeting Rebecca Nove at Jim's Bar. It's right outside the town. She'll be waiting around 11 pm."

"Jim's Bar? The place is called Jim's Bar? Wow. I can't wait to see what their food is like. "

"You'll get to have the nation's finest bug burger."

"They do have other food that isn't bugs right? That's like saying there's only cheesesteaks in Philly."

"Yeah, but if you want extra brownie points you'll try the burger and write up a nice review. Unless you want to keep covering kids playing sports the rest of your career with Times. Come on it won't be so bad if you slather it with ketchup."

"You should eat it then."

"Maybe I will pending your review."

"You got a number or something I can use to call this Nove lady? Maybe get a quote over the phone."

"Oh no, Jack, I'm not giving you shit. I don't want to making up some story and not going."

"I would never."

"Fine, I'll let you know she's a red head and she's not going to be wearing a lab coat."

"Thanks for the cryptic clue."

"She still thinks she's meeting Peggy so be prepared for that."

"Now you tell me. What else is there that I need to know? Is she secretly a minotaur?"

"Jack you know I have other writers to talk to and lots of other work to do. I can't be on the phone all god damn day answering your questions."

"Sorry Sue. I appreciate this. I really do."

"I know, Jack. Don't let me down."

"I won't."

"And Jack?"

"Yeah, Sue?"

"Don't forget to review the burger. You might be able to escape sports just yet."

Jack hung up the phone and set the GPS up for Jim's Bar. If he left now he'd be able to get there by ten.

Driving was the time when the most attention was drawn to having a prosthetic arm. Jack always remembered it was there, but driving was when it came into play. Driving was also the time when he was most grateful for having a prosthetic limb. He kept a black glove over his hand and could open and close it with the remaining nerves he had. There was no amazing way or heroic explanation behind losing his forearm. It happened after a car wreck when he was a kid. His mother was driving and she survived, but he had lost his left arm. He didn't get the prosthetic until he was 18. His parents insurance as many do, won't cover the cost for children to have prosthetic limbs while they're still growing.

He could drive just fine with one hand if he needed to. He learned young to do things with one hand. Prosthetics have come a long way in a short amount of time. He was used to eyes staring at him whenever he went somewhere new. Or hell they would stare even if they had known him.

Women never seemed to mind him having only one arm, staring aside. Not the ones who mattered anyway. They admired his confidence and humor about the situation. He was always willing to give a hand if need be.

He was recently released from a six month stint with a blue haired free spirit. She was someone who pretended to care so much about the world yet missed what was right in front of her. Jack cared about the world too of course. It's a big reason why he wanted to be a journalist. Saving the world through gripping exposes is the half the reason why men become journalists. The other half is women.

Journalists are the least timid of the arts and women can smell it. You can't be a fly on the wall and still get a quote or a story. Poets can observe and dwell about their unrequited love while a journalist takes risks just to write about them. It's self indulgent work but they don't have the luxury of time. They can't hole up for years like a painter can only to produce a red circle on a white canvas as a symbol of their brooding. Journalists have editors breathing down their back demanding content.

Jack finished up the baseball championship story, emailed it to Susan, and headed to a coffee shop to buy enough coffee to keep himself from passing out at the wheel on the way to Clapham.

## CHAPTER 3

Jim's Bar was on the outskirts of Clapham. It featured five tables and a long wrap around bar. It wasn't the most packed bar in the town, but it was the one Rebecca Nove frequented for that reason. She didn't want to be bothered by strangers during the times she managed to have free from studying bugs. Plus she was being bothered plenty enough by those around her that she did know by name. Rebecca sat at the bar tossing a few dried crickets into her mouth between sips of a cold beer. She was only waiting for Jack before she had to resume her duty of watching the stars.

Closest to her where two truckers, Isaac Shaw and Kotto. Shaw was thin with a scraggly beard and Kotto barely had anything hair on his massive frame. Kotto looked like someone had shaved a polar bear. Shaw looked like the type to try shaving a bear.

"You haven't heard from 'em all day?" said Kotto.

"Nope and they clearly ain't here neither," said Shaw.

"But you went by the farm to see?"

"Yeah and there weren't a peep about."

"Maybe they were out back and they couldn't hear you over that music they're always blasting."

"I'm telling you Kotto, there weren't nothing. It was silent. Dead fucking silent."

"What about the crickets?"

"Kotto, it was silent. They weren't making a noise."

"What the fuck you talking about? They always make some noise. Did you go and look to see where they were?"

"I knocked on the house and they didn't answer. The truck wasn't there either."

"What about the crickets?"

"What about 'em?"

"Did you see if there were there?"

"Yeah, I knocked on their little cricket houses and waited for them to open. No I didn't fucking look for the crickets, but I'm telling you there were quiet."

"That's cause crickets are nocturnal, stupid."

"You don't think I know that? Of course I do, but this was different."

"Do you think they're alright?"

"I don't know Kotto."

"I'm sure they're fine. Maybe they went on vacation or took a day trip. I'm sure they'll be back at the bar tomorrow or hell they might pop by tonight."

"I hope you're right, buddy. You know, on the way out of there I hit this armadillo with my truck. It was a big one. I'm talking double the size of any I've ever seen."

"I see more and more of 'em every day. I think it's the nine band invasion."

"The fuck you talking about?"

"Armadillos, they have nine bands, you get it?"

"You keep to driving trucks, Kotto."

Rebecca was pouring beer down her throat when Shaw yelled.

"That's him, that's the guy that killed my wife."

Her head turned to see Shaw standing and pointing at Jack Strafer who had only just walked into the bar.

"Yeah, yeah, the Fugitive. I've heard 'em all. Although I haven't heard that one in ten years. Thanks for the nostalgia trip," said Jack.

Jack took steps into the bar like a newborn calf walking for the first time. His eyes scanned around until he spotted the crimson haired woman. His eyes lowered as he slowly approached her.

"Are you Rebecca Nove?"

"I am, who are you?"

"I'm Jack Strafer."

"Can I help you with something Jack Strafer?"

"I'm looking for Rebecca Nove, I mean I was looking for you. I mean I am looking to meet you. I'm doing a piece about the meteors effect on the bugs."

"Is there something the matter?"

"I guess I thought you'd be-"

"What, white? You ever hear of hair dye? Also I thought it was Betty who was coming, so that's make us even."

"About that, Betty got sick so I'm here-"

"I figured something came up. Hopefully she feels better soon. I've worked with Betty before. She's a hell of a journalist. What made you interested in picking up the story? Bugs or the stars?"

"Guess it's the mix of the two."

She plopped another cricket into her mouth as she waved for two beers.

"Please have a seat," she said.

Jack took the bar stool next to her and the beer greeted him. His eyes followed the next dried cricket as it went from a dish on the counter to Rebecca's mouth.

"You really eat those?"

"No you're imagining it."

"They look disgusting."

"It's just a dried cricket. They're seasoned and barely taste like anything besides the seasoning. Why don't you try one?"

"I'll pass."

"Come on, try it. You're a journalist aren't you? Shouldn't you want to try new things?"

"That doesn't mean I want to eat bugs."

Rebecca took a dried cricket and placed it in Jack's hand. He stared at it. It was covered in a light brown seasoning. Its body was shriveled and its dead eyes looked back at Jack.

"Try it, it's what will save the world."

"You can save the world and I'll report it."

Jack sniffed the cricket and placed it on the counter.

"I thought journalists were meant to be courageous. My sister's a journalist. She was always trying new things just to report about them," she said.

Rebecca took the cricket off the bar and ate it without any hesitation.

"How can you eat them when you study them?" said Jack.

"There's plenty of crickets to study and plenty to eat. Healthier and more humane than killing and eating cows. Crickets don't feel pain."

"I did not know that," he said.

"Maybe you should write some of this down then."

Jack took out his notepad and readied himself to take notes. He asked a few soft questions. *Where she went to school. Why did she choose to study insects. What is the study of insects even called. How much protein is there in bugs compared to traditional meat.*

His note taking was interrupted by one of the truckers. The naked polar bear was throwing crickets to get his attention. Jack turned his head.

"Hey one-arm, get over here," said Kotto.

Jack looked to Rebecca for approval and found none.

"What do you think they want?" said Jack.

"They probably want to give you a hundred bucks," she said.

"Will they shut up if I give in?"

"They might."

Jack walked over to the two truckers who were happily chugging beer.

"What do you want? You going to insult me all night for having one arm?"

"Nah, my buddy Shaw and I are just wondering, where are you from?"

"Texas City."

"No where are you really from?"

"I'm telling you I'm from Texas City. You know, the explosion?"

"No where are you really really from?"

"I'm an American, I don't know what you mean."

"What about your parents?"

"They're from a pacific island."

"Ah, I knew it."

"You've got a real nose there detective,"said Jack.

"Your parents speak English?"

"Probably better than you do."

"I like this guy. What's your name?"

"I'm Jack, Jack Strafer."

"Well Jack Strafer, I'm Kotto," he said extending a hand that Jack shook, "and like I said already, he's Shaw. So what the fuck brings you to this place? You're here to see the bug lady?"

"Bug lady? Isn't this whole town a bunch of bug people?"

"Hey, we only move 'em. We don't look at 'em under a magnifying glass."

"You mean a microscope."

"I don't care either way. Really though, you here to write about the lady who caught the bug bug?"

"Yeah I'm doing a piece about the meteor shower. She's looking into if they effect the crickets and I'm here to see if there's anything worth reporting about it."

"I've seen 'em."

"What the meteors? Big whoop."

"Yeah I see 'em every night up there cutting through the sky. You ever think some disease could come down from the skies and wipe all of humanity out? Something could spread so fast with no creature on Earth having the immunities."

"Can't say I've ever thought about that."

"That's what you should be writing about."

"Who am I supposed to talk to about that?"

"Me of course."

"Sure I'll be back next to get the whole story, how's that sound?"

Jack went back to his stool and found a new man standing by Rebecca. He was tall with a clean shaven face and pale skin. He slouched forward and didn't bother to take a seat. His hands instead were kept on the back of a stool as if they were the only thing keeping him upward.

"So you think the meteors won't possibly affect the bugs? How the fuck would you know that?" said Rebecca.

"Cause I'm an M.D. bitch," he said.

"Is that why you call yourself the midnight doctor? I'm surprised you aren't filming yourself right now. Here to pay a visit before your shift starts?" she said.

"Just a little drink or two to make you look better," he said.

"You're gonna let him talk to you like that?" said Jack.

"Whoa calm down, knight in shining armor," he said.

"Yeah Jack, relax, we've known each other since elementary school," she said.

"I'm guessing you all know each other."

"Pretty much," she said.

The doctor reached into his pocket and handed Jack what looked like a small piece of candy.

"Go ahead, take it," he said.

"What is it?"

"It's a gorilla biscuit," he said before taking out another piece and tossing it into his own mouth.

Jack unraveled his. It was red in color and almost see through. Rebecca smacked his hand from sticking it into his mouth.

"You might want to save that for a time when you don't have to get any writing done," said Rebecca.

Jack pocketed the "biscuit" and took a sip of his beer.

The man walked away leaving the reporter with his subject.

"Don't mind Dr. Sunshower. He's only kidding around."

"That's a weird name."

"Just a little nickname we all call him."

"Why?"

"Cause he'll tell you you have three months to live while eating a sandwich and smiling."

"And what was that you called him? The midnight doctor?"

"Yeah. He likes to do those vlogs. It's what he calls himself when "providing inspiration" to others."

"So he has two nicknames?"

"I guess so."

Sunshower sat down with the truckers and they all raised a glass of beer together. They took a big gulp and let out a laugh towards Rebecca and Jack.

"How have you been doc?" said Shaw.

"Not too bad. Can't say the same for this new influx of patients," said Sunshower.

"There some new cold going round?" said Kotto.

"Certainly something. I heard a few people came in last night barely breathing and covered in sores."

"You sure you should be out here? What if its contagious?"

"Press your luck, Shaw."

"Who's the idiot driving the Ford Pinto?" said a voice walking in.

"That'd be me," said Jack.

It was a police officer in a blue uniform. The name on her shirt read, Ragazza. She stood a little shorter than Jack and looked to be in mid forties with a deep tan.

"And who are you?" she said.

"I'm Jack Strafer, I'm a journalist doing a story about the meteors and Rebecca Nove."

"Well Jesus Christ, Jack Strafer. That must be the last Ford Pinto on Earth. Hell. I thought those were illegal to drive."

"It passed inspection so I think it's fine."

"That's not what I'm talking about, Lefty."

"You do know that makes no sense, right? If anything you should call me Righty."

"Hey calm down, are all your types this high strung?"

"Now what the hell does that mean?"

"You're the journalist here to help out Rebecca, aren't ya?"

"How the fuck do you know that?"

"You've got a notebook bulging out of your pants."

"Ah, right."

"Whatever you're thinking, kid, I'm not one of the bad ones. Now Chief Foro could be classified as such, but I'd never say such a thing while within the confines of his employment. And that's a strict off the record remark. Otherwise I will be what you're thinking. You understand?"

"Got it."

"Good, now how about I buy you a beer."

"I already have one."

"What about a nice cricket burger. Have you had one yet?"

"I'm not sure we have the time," Jack said.

"Of course you do, right Becky?" said Ragazza.

"I bet he's dying to try one," said Rebecca, "I think we have the time."

"It's getting pretty late, we should get to those meteors."

"They can wait, Jack, we have all night," she said.

"Bring us a couple of cricket burgers," said Ragazza.

Ragazza took a seat at a table and waved for Jack and Rebecca to join her. They did and Ragazza tossed a few dried crickets into her mouth.

"How long are you going to be in town Mr. Strafer?" said Ragazza.

"I'm not sure yet. Maybe three or four nights."

"I'm glad you decided to pay our town a visit, but I don't want to interrupt so please continue your conversation," said Ragazza.

"We weren't really talking about much," said Jack.

A server brought a few cricket burgers to the table. Jack lifted the top bun to take a closer inspection. He jotted down a few notes. *Looks normal enough. I'm shocked at how normal actually. The meat looks like a regular burger. I was expecting to see the crickets.*

He dosed it in ketchup and mustard then closed the lid. Slowly the burger came to his mouth and he took a bite. He chewed and let his taste buds become acquainted with the new food. He took another bite and the two women waited for his reaction. The women were already halfway through eating theirs when he finally spoke up.

"It's like a veggie burger, but a little nuttier."

"That's why we're always eating them instead of peanuts. They're healthier for us too."

"Fine, give me one."

Jack looked at the dried cricket again.

"Stop looking at the damn thing and eat it," said Rebecca.

Jack closed his eyes, stuck it on his tongue, and swallowed. A moment later he opened his eyes.

"See? It's no big deal."

"It didn't taste like anything," Jack said.

"No shit, it's what we've trying to tell you."

"I'd still choose beef."

"You get used to it."

"Alright Jack enough socializing with the locals. We need to get out and watch the stars."

"I'm still not exactly sure what you're looking for."

"You'll understand when we're out there."

Jack reached into his wallet for some bills and Ragazza stopped him.

"Don't worry, it's on me. Welcome to Clapham, Jack."

"Thanks. Maybe I'll see you around."

"Probably. Or maybe not, it's only three fucking days."

Rebecca rose from the table and Jack followed her outside. The voices of the truckers, the doctor, and the cop trailed off as they went off into the night.

"Should I drive or?" said Jack.

Rebecca glanced over Jack's car. She could see the pillow, pile of clothes, and books swarming it.

"I'm not getting into that Pinto. You can ride with me."

"Is it alright to leave my car here?"

"As in you think someone will steal it? Or if Jim will care? It's fine Jack. I'll drop you back off when we're done."

She drove a black SUV with heavy tires lifting it higher off the ground than normal. They climbed inside and that's when Jack could hear the crickets chirping in cages in the back seat and trunk. The SUV seemed well furnished even with the cages of insects buckled in.

"Can't be too safe on some of these roads," she said.

"So everyone really calls that guy Sunshower?"

"Yeah even before he was a doctor."

"Does everyone call you bug lady?"

"No, only Shaw and Kotto do that," she said laughing.

"Is everyone in this town nuts or is it just because I'm an outsider?"

"They all mean well."

"I'm not so sure."

"Where the hell are we headed anyway?"

"The woods."

CHAPTER 4

They had been driving for about fifteen minutes when Rebecca pulled the car over to the side of the road. The dark night sky was clear and they were seemingly alone with the trees. Both sides of the road were covered in foliage. Rebecca turned to Jack with a grin before climbing out of the car.

"You ready for some fun?" she said.

"Yeah I'm actually a little excited to see the meteors. It's not often I get to see the stars like this without light pollution," he said.

"Oh we're not going to be able to see the meteors through the woods," said Rebecca.

Jack took a breath then followed her out to the back of the SUV. The hatch opened to show two cages filled with crickets. Tight crisscrossed wire made up of the bulk of the cage with a small handle on top. Rebecca handed Jack two of the cages, turned his head and she was suddenly gone. He ran cages with hand around to the front of the car, but Rebecca wasn't there. He ran towards to the right side of the wooded road and saw nothing. The crickets chirps increased as he made his way back across.

"Over here," she said.

She was standing by a tall thick oak tree still holding a bundle of cord in her hand.

"You better be careful you don't get lost out here. And we're barely in the woods."

Jack took a breath when he reached her.

"Hey, you can relax when we're finished. Now put that cage up in this tree."

"You want me to do it?"

"You didn't think you were going to carry those crickets around all night, did you?"

Jack put one cage down and heaved the other onto a hearty branch. Rebecca handed him some chord and he slung it through the handle and wrapped it around the cage tying it to the tree.

"What about the other one?"

"You can leave it on the ground."

"Really?"

"Yes Jack."

"Now what?"

"I monitor their reaction."

"And how is this important to science? We're not seeing anything. There's nothing happening."

"Given the Perseids happen yearly and insects are the future of food, I'd say it's important Jack."

"Who funded this crap?"

"The university."

"Is it my tax dollars?"

"No you absolute moron."

Jack took out his notepad and got ready to scribble down quotes.

"Alright, what sort of reaction are you looking for?"

"My hypothesis is that mild traces of radiation could affect the insect population. Now normally that wouldn't matter over a normal town. But we have such a massive insect population that it's possible these meteors could affect our food."

"How the hell would a cricket even know what a meteor is?"

Rebecca sat on the ground and Jack stood by the tree examining the cage crickets. There were just enough gaps in the trees to see the meteors flying above. One zipped by and the crickets chirps increased. Rebecca smiled.

"That's not entirely what I meant, but it does help prove my point," she said, "I meant it more as the falling meteors could go into the ground, grass grows over it and the insects eat the grass."

"Aren't the insects farmed?"

"Yes Jack, we're not eating wild crickets, but the grass we feed them does come from this town. This town where the meteors fall more readily. You're really bad at connecting dots for a journalist."

"So then why bring out cages of them if you want to see how it affects grass?"

"Because they just got louder. And they always chirp louder when the meteors come. And I want to know why, Jack. I have a Geiger counter in each cage for good measure. And to see if it picks up on the meteors affecting bigger plant life such as trees."

"Maybe the meteors make a sound that the crickets can hear?"

"That's not a bad theory. If it keeps happening then there might be something to it."

"We saw it happen already. How much equipment would you want to drag out here to prove it?"

"Scientists have to be objective Jack. Surely you as a journalist can understand that."

"Really? I always thought you only took evidence that supports your hypothesis."

"Do you even know what a hypothesis is?"

"Of course I do. It's your end goal you'll do anything to meet. You need more funding after all."

"It's true they expect something resembling what they want, but that's how it is with everything. What's your usual beat Jack?

"Sports."

"And you need to placate to those who want to read a sports story right? Most of the time it's a brief summary of the game. Sure there's a rare deep story, but as I said, most of the time it's fluff."

"Sports is real news. Most of the people, men and women alike, in my classes wanted to cover sports."

"And what about you? Do you enjoy covering sports?"

"It pays the bills."

"Yeah you're doing real well living in your car, but hell, Jack, that isn't what I asked."

"I was never the biggest sports fan. If you hadn't noticed I'm not the most athletic type."

"That's bullshit, Ever hear of the special Olympics?"

"I guess not everyone wants to be an athlete."

"That's fair enough. How about this? You don't insult what I do and I won't insult what you do," she said.

Rebecca reached into her pocket and pulled out a few dried crickets. She tossed them into her mouth and a dried leg fell out.

"Do you think they mind?"

"Of course they don't mind."

"It's just that you never saw Jane Goodall eating chimp jerky while hanging out with the apes."

"I guess you're on to something there."

"Hey let me ask you, what's up with that cop's last name?"

"Raggaza?"

"Yeah, it means girl in Italian."

"So?"

"What kind of last name is that?"

"Maybe she comes from a long line of women."

"That doesn't make sense. If there were only women then how could the name spread? And if there were more than women, the name would get married out."

"Not if the tradition is for the men to take the name."

"It still sounds like something a bad writer would come up with."

"What about you?" What kind of name is Strafer?"

"My family were assigned it during WWII."

"I wonder Jack, would you be saying all this if she were a man? You're off to a bad start in your career if you're being sexist."

"I'm not sexist. I'm curious, which journalists should be."

"You're also bad at detecting sarcasm. That's an even worse start."

"Hey. It takes time for me to tell when someone is kidding or not."

"That needs to change. The sooner the better."

"Kidding, right?"

"No," she said before cracking a small laugh.

They settled down on a few lawn chairs and stared up at the trees around them. Jack continued to reject the multiple offers of dried crickets as a snack.

"How long do you usually stay out?"

"Only a few hours."

"And you sit here the entire time?"

"No I go for walks and come back."

"But what about monitoring the crickets?"

"The cages are bugged."

"I bet you've always wanted to say that."

"Never had the opportunity until now."

"How about we go for a walk and I'll ask some more questions?"

Rebecca rose and waved for Jack to follow. They left behind the cages and stepped deeper into the woods. A light was shining through the trees about thirty yards from where they left their car.

"Is there a road through here?" said Jack.

"No, maybe it's campers," said Rebecca.

"Should we say hi? Maybe I could interview them about living in a bug town."

"I thought you were going to interview me?"

"I'll have plenty of time now that I know I'm spending three nights listening to crickets bark at meteors."

"Hey it's your job," she said, "But I'm going to stay back. If it's those farmers I don't want them to see me."

"What farmers?"

"There's a family that lives out here who don't like me very much."

"Who wouldn't like you? I've known you for only a few hours and you've only repeatedly insulted me."

Jack walked over to find the source of the lights. It was a truck. It was upside down and crinkled, but Jack could still tell it was a truck. Jack used his cell phone's flashlight to take a closer look. The headlights were smashed with glass and pieces of metal scattered around. *How the hell could the battery still be working? Maybe an animal turned it on.* He switched to his phone's camera and snapped a few pictures with the flash.

"Rebecca, you might want to come see this," Jack yelled back.

She appeared a few seconds later with her own cellphone light shining.

"It's their truck alright, the farmers," she said.

"They must have had an accident," I said, "but I don't see any bodies."

"That'd be one hell of an accident to have their car flipped and crushed like an accordion."

"Do you think they did it themselves?"

"Are you asking if I think a couple of farmers took their truck, their livelihood, flipped it, and smashed it? Why the hell would they do that?"

"I don't know, for the insurance money?"

"No Jack, but I don't know what the fuck happened. They weren't ones to take their truck off road for mudding."

"I'm going to take a look around," he said.

Jack went into the woods holding his phone high then low as if he were examining every leaf for evidence. He was barely within ear range when he heard Rebecca scream his name. He ran through the woods towards the scream until he found her standing in the dark with her phone off.

"What?" he said, "Are you alright?"

"For fuck's sake, no, I'm not alright," she said, "Its's-he's."

"What?"

She grabbed Jack's hand that was holding the cell phone and pointed it to the ground a few feet from where they were standing. Jack's light shone on the area and on the ground was a headless corpse wearing overalls. Flies were swarming where the head once was. Bugs ants swarmed the open wound and the bloated skin. Jack covered his mouth with his good arm to fight back from emptying his stomach of the cricket burger onto the ground.

"That's Karl, I know it," she said.

Her voice was broken, but she held back any tears.

"Where's his fucking head?" she said.

"Maybe he lost it in the accident? It could be in the woods somewhere."

Jack flashed his phone around their perimeter seeing only trees in his light. He took a few photos of the headless man.

"Stop that," she said.

"What the fuck should we do? I need these photos for evidence," he said.

"We need to call for help for sure."

"The cops?"

"I don't know. Maybe we should call his brother or sister."

"Do you have their number?"

"No, but they live close by."

"I think we should just call the cops."

"Alright, but let's get back to my car first. I need a moment."

Jack led the way back to the car with his phone held high. They left behind the truck and the headless corpse.

Rebecca's feet tried to take another step, but they were firmed planted on the ground. She took her phone out and shine down seeing her feet wrapped in a black tar substance.

"Jack!"

His head whipped back to see Rebecca squirming to free herself from the black goo. Jack extended his prosthetic arm towards her. She latched on and he yanked her away from the tar.

"What the hell is it?" he said.

"I don't know, but it smells horrible," she said.

Rebecca took a fresh fallen branch and poked at the goo on the ground.

A piece of white stuck out from the black. The stick hooked the white and pulled it out from the tar. Rebecca plopped it onto the grass and Jack couldn't help but vomit next to it.

It was a skull. The teeth were covered in black and looked rotted, but there was no doubt that it was a skull. A human skull with two pools of black with the eyes once were and a hole where the nose should be. Pieces of skin still clung around the cheeks and the top of the head had a few stray hairs who didn't give up the fight.

Jack wiped his mouth and tried to regain his composure. He snapped another couple pictures.

"You think it's another farmer?"

"It's his brother, Bill. Jesus Christ, what the fuck happened?"

"I'm starting to think this wasn't an accident, Rebecca."

"We need to get out of here now," she said.

"You don't have to tell me that, let's go."

Rebecca and Jack ran full sprint back to the SUV.

"Fuck, I can't leave the crickets," she said.

"I'll go get them," he said.

Jack turned back, untied the cage and brought it back to the ground. He picked up the cage and started back for the car when he smelled the same stench. He placed both cages down and vomited again after what he saw. He stood in disbelief for at least thirty seconds which is when Rebecca came over to him.

"Jack come on, what are you doing?"

"You said there was a sister right?"

"Yeah?"

"I think I just found her."

Rebecca looked over Jack's shoulder to see a pile of sludge on the ground. It was the same black tar with a horrid stench that she was caught in. A thin arm protruded out from the mass. Its hand was out stretched towards a messy long glob of goo.

Rebecca had to hold back her own vomit and swallowed profusely to keep a diet of dried crickets from resurfacing.

"What the fuck is going on?" she said.

"What's she reaching for?" said Jack.

"I don't know, grab it," she said.

"You grab it," he said.

Rebecca reached into the black and pulled out a covered shotgun. It looked rusted and as if it hadn't been fired in a century. It dripped the black tar onto the ground and the stock fell off.

"There's no way that's their regular gun," he said.

Rebecca wiped her hands on her pants. Jack took a photo of the rotted gun and the black tar covered body with the grabbing arm.

"Fuck this stuff burns," she said.

Rebecca headed back to the car as Jack followed with his cell phone beaming everywhere. He took a few steps deeper into the woods away from the SUV.

"Rebecca, wait," he said, "You should see this."

"Jesus Christ, what now? The entire family is fucking dead, Jack, there's no one left to be dead out here," she said.

"It's not a body," he said.

He shined his phone down on the ground for Rebecca to see. A gigantic footprint had indented the ground. It was at least five feet wide and two feet deep. There were clearly impressions of five toes. Jack took some more photos before sliding the phone into his pocket.

"What the fuck is going? Is there a goddamn T.Rex on the loose?" said Jack.

"I don't know, I've never seen anything like this before," she said.

"That's impossible right? Nothing could be this big and support its own weight," he said.

"The square cube law would agree with you there Jack, but reality seems to be arguing with you both."

"Something this big shouldn't be able to hide."

"Again, I agree with you, but clearly this thing is no where to be found."

He picked up the cages and put them in the back of the SUV. Jack climbed into the passenger seat to Rebecca holding her sneakers and intently staring at the bottom of them.

"Jack, it's my shoes. The soles are completely melted. That stuff must be some sort of acid."

"That would explain the rotten corpses and ancient gun. What should we do now?"

"I guess we're going to go tell the chief. You took the photos, he has to believe us. We may need to quarantine the entire town. We can't have people touching this stuff. Not to mention there's a goddamn giant monster walking around."

"I don't know the guy, but he's going to think we're fucking nuts."

"We have to tell someone Jack, we can't let others die."

"I guess the bright side is this going to be one hell of a story."

## CHAPTER 5

Dr. Sunshower was cruising in the parking lot of the hospital. He had a new mustang he drove to show off how luxurious his life has become since becoming a resident at the hospital. He made it and could stay comfortable here until he died. He intended to do just that. The hospital held only a hundred beds. That meant there was never much of a crisis. Nothing that he and the other two docs on staff with their nurses doing most of the heavy lifting couldn't handle.

His fingers drummed on the wheel as he pulled into his personal parking spot.

The doctor had a decent following on social media. His biggest was through Snap Chat. Thousands watched his motivational videos. The man in a car videos were hotter than ever and his numbers showed it.  Rebecca Nove had given him shit for it on multiple occasions. Worth shit giving considering he'd sometimes start a video while he was still driving.

But he was parked now with five minutes to spare before heading into his shift. The phone zipped out from his pocket and his voice boomed from the car into the internet.

"I'm the midnight doctor, coming to you once again to give you all out there on the night shift a little pep talk. When life gets you down just believe in yourself. It starts with a small change. I never thought I'd be a doctor, but here I am. And here you are. You can do it. All of you out there working the nights with me, we're a special breed. We don't get the sunshine, but we do get the starlight. And for all of you who can see the sky, now's a good time to look up. The meteors are zipping like crazy up there. Take care of yourselves and I'll see you on the next snap."

A flood of thumbs up overtook his phone.

He unraveled a gorilla biscuit from his pocket and looked down at it.

It looked like a hard piece of candy. You wouldn't be able to tell it wasn't some no name brand from a dollar store. That was on purpose. There was even the local tradition of putting a cricket right into the candy.

He wouldn't be getting blitzed. There would be no hallucinations. They helped to take the edge of. That's all. A little something to help him get through the shift. These were the things he told himself anyway. It wasn't a one doc town or anything but the stress of being a doctor is enough whether there's more on staff or not. The night shift had three. He was one of them. While he enjoyed the work it was stressful no matter what.

The doctor took a deep breath before plopping the treat into his mouth and reaching for the door handle.

He could tell something was off the moment he stepped inside.

His favorite nurse, Ms. Denham, wasn't there to brief him. She was usually awaiting his arrival. Not just because they slept together in spare beds, but because she understood him better than anyone in the hospital. Sunshower and her made a great team. And to go into work without your partner there is enough to start the anxiety engines.

He found her down the hallway standing at a vending machine trying to shake quarters out of her scrubs. Sunshower went up and wrapped his arm around her waist.

"K.C., we can't tonight," she said.

"Why not?"

"We have fifteen patients tonight."

"What the fuck? Fifteen? Why? It's way too early for flu season."

"It's not the flu, it's something else. Don't you smell it? It's those people who came in last night. There's more of them."

"I figured we had a toilet problem or something."

"It's the patients, I can barely stay in a room with them."

"So let's find an empty room for ourselves."

"I'm serious, we need to figure out what's wrong with them."

"Wait, you don't know?"

"I just told you, it's something else. I don't know what it is yet."

"What'd Sandman say?"

"He took the night off."

"And Chelsea?"

"Now her kid actually has the flu."

"That's fucking great. This is fucking great. Are you saying I'm the only doctor in tonight?"

"That shouldn't be a problem for the midnight doctor, right?"

"You catch tonight's message?"

"No, I've been in here waiting for your dumb ass to show up. You got anything to take the edge off?"

He tossed her a wrapped biscuit and she quickly ate it.

"I need a smoke, you should go into room 17 first," she said.

Sunshower walked to the room and inside lay an older woman. She was barely conscious as he approached the bed. There was a strange smell in the air. It was rotten and stunk of garbage he hadn't smelled since his days in college. Her body was covered in bumps and her skin looked stained black. It's as if someone took magic maker to her body and then tried to scrub it off. He picked up the file.

Janus Wilkins, DOB 4/26/1950.

The old woman opened her eyes, but didn't say a word. Her eyes looked like they could burst into tears at any moment. Still she held strong and not a drop came out.

"Oh you're awake? How are you feeling Mrs. Wilkins?"

She laid motionless. Yes her eyes were open and she seemed awake, but she wasn't moving at all. Her eyes themselves stared forward. They didn't dart around confused. They didn't even blink. They were open. They were still.

"It's alright you don't have to talk. Keep resting. I didn't mean to wake you up."

"She's been like that since she got in," said Nurse Denham in the doorway.

"Has she said anything?"

"Not a word. You might want to check out room 19 now. There's a man laying in there. He was awake and talking as of ten minutes ago. He's the one who found the old woman."

"You mean she was found? Where?"

"Go ask him, Sunny" she said.

Sunshower walked finding a young man laying in the bed. His skin was reddish. Not of ancestral descent. This was an unnatural red coloring to his skin similar to the blackening of the older woman.

"Nurse Denham informed me that you found that old woman."

"Yeah she was outside the Shop-Mart near her car. I work there. At the Shop-Mart and I park far out. I guess she does too. Don't want to get hit by any idiots, right? Well she was there collapsed and covered in this black goo. I picked her up, put her in my truck and brought her here."

"Did she say anything to you?"

"No, doc, she didn't say a word."

"Alright, hopefully she'll talk soon. But that leaves me with another question."

"What's that doc?"

"If you found the old woman and you were fine before, why are you in a hospital bed now?"

"I'm not feeling too good, doc. I'm not feeling too good at all."

"I can't help you unless you tell me what's wrong. I assume you're not typically this red, right?"

"I'm red?"

"All over. Looks you were covered in blisters and scratched them open."

"I don't know doc. My hands are feeling real numb. My legs and feet too. It's like I can barely feel my body at all. I'm scared doc. What the hell is happening to me?"

"I'm not sure yet myself Mr.-"

"Mr. Gerald," he said.

"Stay put Mr. Gerald. We'll find out what's wrong."

"You don't think I got it from her, do you doc? I don't want some black goo disease."

"It's too early to tell," Sunshower said.

His moniker meant he never felt remorse in telling his patients bad news. He didn't know what to tell Mr. Gerald. He could face telling a man he had cancer, but the unknown scared him.

"We have another patient inbound," she said.

Sunshower turned to see Denham standing in the door again.

"What's wrong with 'em?"

"Same thing, Sun," she said, "This one still is covered in that black crap."

She led him to the waiting room where the new patients sat. Sure enough a man had his leg covered in some black goo-like substance. He wasn't alone. There was a young woman beside him.

"What happened? Where is all this crap coming from? What the hell are you people doing?" Sunshower said.

"I was on the side of the road when I heard this sound and I looked up to see a meteor falling just as I stepped out. Anyway there was this shit all over the place and I got stuck in it."

"Why would you come to the hospital over getting caught in some sticky mud?"

"It feels like its burning doc," he said.

"Why didn't you take it off?"

"Don't you think I would have if I could?"

"Nurse, please help him clean off his leg,"

There was another nurse besides Denham working of course. He took the man back into a room and began clearing him of the tar.

"Try to get a sample of that crap too," said Sunshower as they walked away, "And wear gloves!"

"And what about you?" he said towards the woman, "How are you feeling? Did you touch that stuff too?"

"I'm feeling fine. I just brought him in because he couldn't drive with his leg bothering him."

"Are you sure you're feeling okay?"

"I might have a cold coming on, but it could just be allergies," she said.

"Keep a nurse noted on how you're feeling, alright?"

"Don't you think we should be more focused on him?"

"We're going to keep a good eye on him. I want to make sure you're feeling fine."

"I feel fine, honest. I was hoping I could go back home," she said.

"It might be better for you to stick around a little. You don't know when he's going to get done after all."

"Okay, Sunshower, I can stick around," she said.

Everyone in town knew him by that name. She knew to stick around when he said to, too. The doctor walked back past the vending machine where he found Denham at the start of the shift. She was the one to grab him this time.

"What do you think of all this?" she said.

"I don't know. Some sort of disease spreading through them. I don't know if it's person to person or from contact with that black stuff."

"You know what it reminds me of?"

"Does it look like we have time for guessing games?" he said.

"I just thought maybe you'd want to make the diagnosis yourself, doc. It looks like leprosy to me."

"I thought of that, but leprosy shouldn't be this contagious. Leprosy doesn't consume someone in a matter of hours like it did that old woman."

"I know. Normally it'd take months for it to spread over, but the symptoms are the same. There numbness, the blisters, the reddening of the skin. Anyone would think it's leprosy if they didn't know the time line."

"Okay, let's say it is leprosy. There's a cure for that. Start them all on a treatment."

"Are you sure?"

"I don't have any better ideas. We can at least rule out leprosy if it doesn't work."

The nurse who took the man with the leg problem came into the hallway.

"Don't you hear it?"

"Hear what?"

"Ms. Wilkin's room, she's flatlining."

Sunshower and Denham ran to the old woman's room and found her there, eyes open. Not only were they still open, but they were black and rotting. The same tar was running out her tear ducts. She had finally cried.

"She said something," a voice said.

Sunshower and Denham turned to see Mr. Gerald sitting in the corner.

"What?" said Sunshower.

"Before she went, she said something," Mr. Gerald said.

"Well? What did she say?" asked Denham.

"Armadillo," he said.

"As in the animal?" asked Sunshower.

"I guess. It's all she said. One word, armadillo."

"Armadillo? Who knows what was going on in her mind in her last moments. Maybe she saw an armadillo in the room in her mind. Maybe she has one as a pet."

The old woman's body started to convulse. It was as if she was having a seizure. The doctor and nurse would easily recognize it as such if Ms. Wilkins hadn't just died. It soon slowed to an almost too calm for a regular seizure. Her arms and legs were vibrating. You could see them moving under the blanket, but it was subtle. A moment later her head popped. The black substance grenaded throughout the bed. The smell nearly took the dinner out of Sunshower. Denham looked under the blanket and her entire body had turned to mush. The tar engulfed it all and there would be little proof she ever came to the hospital had they not been there to see it.

"What the hell are we dealing with here, doc?" said Mr. Gerald.

"I don't know yet. You have to stay here. Get back to your room."

"Is that going to happen to me?"

"No, no, you're going to be just fine."

It was the first time he had lied while at work. The first lie of comfort he ever gave to a patient he knew wasn't going to make it.

Sunshower and Denham walked out to talk privately in the hallway.

"Leprosy doesn't make your body pop like a grease filled balloon."

"I don't think we're dealing with regular leprosy here.

"Why do you look like you're headed out somewhere?" she said.

"I need to go tell the Chief we have an outbreak of something."

"What you're going to tell him there's super leprosy? He'll laugh in your face."

"Why would you say that?"

"Because I already called him, Sun."

"You did what? Why? When?"

"When you were checking on that man with the covered leg."

"And he laughed at you?"

"Everything but. He wants proof before he can issue any quarantine."

"Should I scoop Ms. Wilkins into a jar for him?"

"That'd be disgusting, but it might be what he needs to see."

"He could have been here to see it and he would still not want a quarantine."

"Maybe if we can talk to him in person he'll understand. We've got to try, dammit."

"Sun? I'm not feeling so great myself. You better go by yourself," she said.

She pulled up her sleeve and her left arm was reddened. A large blister was forming on the inside of her elbow.

"Christ, it must be person to person. You didn't touch the goo, right?"

"No, I didn't," she said.

"Start yourself on a leprosy treatment. I'll be back. If patients come in that don't have serious illnesses, turn them away. Better make one of the other nurses do it. Even better is you get into a bed."

"I'm not going to lie down and die while I can still help."

"Fine. Stick to the other super lepers."

"I'm not going to dissolve, am I?"

"No of course not."

Another lie. He had never wanted to start lying because he knew how easy it would be to keep at it.

Sunshower climbed back into his mustang. He sighed and took out his phone.

"Hey there folks, the midnight doctor is here to give you a very special message. There's a real nasty bug going around. You don't want this little sickness, kids. Stay inside if you can. Take this time to work on yourselves. Do some meditating or reading. Take the time to get acquainted with your introverted side. I'm only venturing out to help those who can't be helped. Stay safe, stay motivated and take care."

## CHAPTER 6

Kotto was leading ahead in the road. His truck was hauling 60,000 pounds of crickets. Those chirpers were luckily unheard given the soundproofing of the trailer. Truckers would go mad if they had to listen to the chorus of a million bugs. But Kotto didn't have to and he didn't care what he was transporting. The jobs around here paid better than anything before he'd done. *It might be a bug town, but it's the best damn bug town I've ever been to.* He'd say over beers. It's something he wanted to say to that new face. Maybe he would the next time he saw him. That man with the one arm.

The roads to Clapham were wide and empty. Not much was out here during the night. Traffic was fine during the day, but when the sun set it seemed no one went anywhere. They had no where to go. The regulars at Jim's Bar weren't enough to make much of a flow. Luckily the town did install lampposts down the highway. A little bit of light was something during the lonely nights on the road.

Isaac Shaw, the thin man, was following behind Kotto's rig. Shaw's own trailer only carried half the insects of Kotto's. He'd been working out here longer than Kotto had. His entire family came from the transporting of goods. He was a generational trucker and didn't want anything different. All the bugs you could eat and the company even gave out houses to those who worked for 'em.

They were taking their hauls into the town. A factory took care of all the bug manufacturing in Clapham. No one cared if the single company had a monopoly. They paid well enough to everybody in the town. It's as if the whole town worked for the company and the company worked for them. It was one big organism working together to support itself.

Trucks ran all day and all night. The demand for bugs was increasing at a rate that the company could barely keep up with. Kotto and Shaw always met up at the bar for a few drinks before completing their route to the factory.

"You've been quiet all trip," said Kotto into the radio.

"I haven't had much to say is all," said Shaw.

"There something you want to talk about?"

"What are you? My wife? I don't want to talk about shit with you Kotto, you talking walrus."

"You're worried about the farmers. It's alright. I am too."

"I'm not worried about the farmers. They're probably off on a vacation."

"But if they aren't, you're worried. You don't want that girlfriend of yours slipping away."

"She wasn't my girlfriend."

"Didn't you go on a few dates?"

"We didn't date."

"That's not how I remember it. I don't know why you're shy about it anyway. She wasn't that ugly."

"We slept together during a power outage. That's all. Can we drop the subject now?"

"You want to spend another half hour in total silence?"

"You want to hear something? You want something to kill the awkward silence? Open the back flap up. Listen to the orchestra you're hauling."

"No need to get all pissy about shit. Let me apologize for considering your feelings on the matter of a lost loved one. Fine, I won't mention her again. Her or her giant tits."

"She doesn't have giant tits."

"The fuck you mean? There was no hiding those things whenever she were around."

"Maybe if you were holding a magnifying glass."

"Come on man, I know you know what I'm talking about. Aren't we talking about Sadie?"

"Sadie? I saw Sadie earlier today. She's fine. Judy's the one missing. Her and her damned brothers."

"Oh Judy, yeah she was flat as a board. Still she wasn't too bad. And excuse me for the confusion. They all got brothers, Isaac. You can't expect me to keep track of 'em all."

Shaw's truck began to rumble. His cabin was vibrating and he gripped the wheel to keep the whole thing from tipping over. He screamed into the radio.

"What's going on?"

"Earthquake?" said Kotto.

"There's no earthquakes here."

"Judgment day then, friend."

The earth itself was shaking. Shaw could see Kotto's trailer ahead. It was zig-zagging back and forth like a dog happy to see its owner.

"You okay up there?"

"It's only a little ground turbulence. Now who's worried about who? It's nice to see you concerned about something."

The quaking wasn't letting up. Shaw held onto the wheel and let the radio drop. He could hear Kotto's voice still chattering away.

"You okay back there?"

The lines in the road began to peel up. The Earth was lifting. Kotto's mother had warned him as a child of the Judgment Day. When God would tear apart the Earth and those ridden with sin would be drug down into the depths of Hell.

It turned into a storm of concrete, asphalt, and dirt. Grass from the side of the road was thrown into the mix. Shaw slammed on the brakes to keep the truck from falling into the massive hole before him. Not that he knew it was a hole. He braked to keep from going deeper into the shit storm. Kotto slammed his own truck sending it to a sideways stop.

"What the fuck is going on?" shouted Kotto through the radio, "Shaw you still with me?"

Shaw bent down to pick his receiver back up.

"I don't know. This ain't like any quake I've ever heard of or been in. Are you alright?" said Shaw.

"It was close back there, but I think everything's alright. Did you get a look at it?"

"At the earthquake? I definitely felt it."

"Forget about the earthquake, Shaw. You seeing this right now?"

"Seeing what? I can barely see anything through all this goddamn dust."

Shaw lifted back up and used his wipers to clear off the windshield of the truck. The dust was beginning to clear and through the lights of the lamp posts, Shaw could see it. It was still mostly in the ground. A big shadow of a beast. A plated humped back was the bulk of his eyesight. The Armordillo had its front claws out and its long snout was sniffing the air. Shaw could see a profile view of its head. It's nose was pointed to Kotto's truck.

"Jesus Christ, what is that thing?"

"You know what it is."

"If you're telling me it's an armadillo, I'm telling you, you're out of your mind. Armadillos don't get that big."

"Guess we're both hallucinating the biggest goddamn armadillo to ever live then."

"What do you think it wants?"

"You know how you said tonight that you've hit a few armadillos in your truck? Maybe they sent they're biggest guy out on revenge."

"You're joking."

"Yeah, but we're gonna need a bigger truck."

"How long have you been waiting to say that?"

"Would you believe it just came to me? The big guy probably wants some food."

"What do armadillos eat anyway?"

"Insects. What the fuck did you think they eat?"

"I don't know. I never thought about it. Who the fuck thinks about what armadillos eat?"

"I'm pretty sure they eat crickets and this big fucker probably smells the shit ton we're carrying."

"I think we should get out of here."

"Why? It's not doing anything."

"You don't know that."

"And where are you going to go? You can't get past the hole it made in the ground."

It was true to some extent. The dust cleared and Shaw could see the Armordillo was still looking around and sniffing the air. It didn't seem to pose any immediate threat.

"I could go around it."

"Are you nuts? That'd only provoke it. Don't give it a reason to attack us."

Shaw shifted the truck into reverse and slowly backed up. He kept an eye on the Armordillo and it wasn't moving. He was in the middle of a K turn when he saw Kotto being Kotto.

Shaw hit the brakes when he saw the heavy bald man climbing down from his rig. He rolled down his window to yell at him.

"What the fuck are you getting out of your truck for?" said Shaw.

"I'm going to get a picture."

"Are you out of your fucking mind?"

Kotto gave a hearty laugh and waved as he stepped towards the massive armadillo.

The beast lifted itself from the hole. It stomped on all fours as it walked towards Kotto's truck. Shaw could see it wasn't an ordinary armadillo. Of course anyone could see that from size alone. But size aside, Shaw could see it was different. The plating seemed thicker. It didn't look organic. It truly looked like an armadillo wearing armor. Even a truck twice its size would have trouble squishing it with all that protection.

Shaw hopped out of his own truck and watched from across the hole.

The Armordillo sunk its claws into the side of the trailer. Shaw covered his ears over in feign attempt to block out the sound of metal screeching as it was torn. It's tongue popped out and began licking the insides like an ice cream cone. Hundreds of crickets were consumed by the second. Some crickets jumped out of its mouth only to be eaten a moment later. It seemed to have no end to its appetite. Pieces of the metal cage would fall out in between bites. They hit the ground like raindrops and Kotto left out a laugh. He slowly crept towards the Armordillo and turned to yell towards Shaw.

"I don't think it even sees us," said Kotto.

Shaw didn't say anything in response. He stood like a pillar watching the monstrous armadillo devour cricket after cricket. He could hear the pleading chirps. *They were going to be food anyway, but not like this.*

"That motherfucker is cracking open my trailer like it were a cold one. I guess it's a good thing I got out of my truck, isn't it?" said Kotto.

"Sure, yeah. But now you should get away from there," said Shaw.

"Are you kidding me? I gotta put this shit on youtube man, people gonna love this shit."

"Get the hell away from there Kotto," shouted Shaw.

"Calm down, I just want a closer look. No one will believe this."

The Armordillo's head poked out from the torn trailer. It's long tongue licked its armored lips and it held a look of smug satisfaction on its face. Shaw would say it almost looked happy if his father never told him that animals never felt nothing. This one definitely did though.

Kotto moved in closer, holding the phone up to try and get a picture.

"It's too damn dark out. Fuckers put these lamp posts out here for nothing."

"Kotto, get the fuck out of there," Shaw shouted louder.

"Don't be such a baby. All it wanted was a snack. It's going to be one hell of a story to tell the guys at Jim's, ain't it Shaw?"

The Armordillo sniffed the air again. It looked down to see the large hairless man pointing a strange object at it. A claw came swinging down at the trucker. Shaw had never seen Kotto move so fast in his life. The human walrus jumped out of the way and fell to the ground. He was cracking up with laughter, rolling around on the torn earth. His phone was sent flying and the Armordillo stepped on the device.

"Kotto!"

Shaw ran towards to the beast and his friend. The Armordillo bent down and grabbed the fallen Kotto with its other claw. Shaw paused ten feet away near the hole the creature emerged from.

"Shaw, get this thing off me!"

Kotto wasn't laughing anymore. He pounded his heavy fists down on the claws he was gripped in. A crunching sound was heard in retaliation. The Armordillo had squeezed back. Shaw could see the large man go limp and his struggle was over.

Shaw watched as the creature slowly ate his coworker and friend. The tongue wrapped around Kotto's left arm yanked it clean off. Blood trickled out and the Armordillo held the body up to let the blood fall right into its mouth. Shaw saw the color fade from his friend's body. He soon became pale and the Armordillo bit his head off with a pop. Then it tossed the body on the ground like it were an empty bottle of beer.

Kotto had become the dessert to the meal that was a trailer full of crickets.

Shaw stood there frozen. He didn't know what to do. His legs wouldn't move. How could he get revenge for his friend? His friend had been an idiot until the end, but he was still a friend. He was a human with thoughts and feelings and Shaw had to make this thing pay.

*I've got to call 911.*

He reached into his pocket, but his phone wasn't there. *Fuck, it's probably in the goddamn cabin. And Kotto's is smashed on the ground.*

They didn't have any guns in their trucks. The company didn't allow it. Not that they ever needed them. They weren't farmers. They normally never worried about anything attacking their cargo like a farmer would their farm.

The Armordillo turned its attention back to the scrounging up the remaining crickets in Kotto's trailer.

*Fuck it. I've got to get out of here. I've got to tell the Chief. Tell him what? That a giant armadillo just killed Kotto? He's going to think I'm insane.*

He slowly backed up keeping his eye on the Armordillo until he was far enough away to make a run for it. His legs seemed to working now. He dashed into the woods and climbed up on a hill. Shaw glanced back to see the Armordillo making its way over to his own trailer. *This motherfucker is still wanting to eat?* The same screech was heard. This time he was already far enough away that it didn't pierce his ears. But there was no mistaking the sound of thousands of crickets being devoured in seconds. The chorus of dying bugs rang out into the night. If he ran he could make it to the police station within a half hour. *Better make it forty-five.* He briskly headed to meet with the Chief.

CHAPTER 7

Deputy Ragazza was sitting at her desk in the police station when they walked in. Paperwork was her least favorite part of the job. She'd take any excuse not to do it. So she personally waved over the journalist and scientist after seeing another officer grow annoyed with them. Seeing when people walked in was perhaps the only perk to not having her own office despite being deputy.

They shambled over with wide eyes and frazzled hair. The other officer gave a shrug and returned to looking at his computer.

"You've been in town a night and already causing trouble Mr. Strafer?" said Ragazza.

Jack Strafer straightened his posture and flexed his prosthetic arm.

"Hardly. I'm only reporting on it," he said.

"Relax a little Strafer. But you know you shouldn't come to my work if you want to hang out. That's what Jim's is for."

"We're not here to hang out," said Jack.

"It's important," said Rebecca.

Ragazza took a sip of her coffee and leaned back.

"It better be if I'm the one handling it. What brings you in then? How can I help you two?"

"There were these bodies and these footprints and this black goo," said Jack.

"Alright, hold on. If you found some bodies you're going to need to start from the beginning. Where were you two at?"

"At the woods near the brothers farm," said Rebecca.

"What the hell were you doing out there. Isn't that private property?"

"Their farm might be, but not the woods outside of it. They only tell people that so they stay away. That's not the point. The point is they're gone. They're dead."

"They're the bodies you found?"

"Hello? Are you listening Ragazza? I know you're not this dumb," said Rebecca.

"I know we're friends, but you can't talk to me like that," said Ragazza.

"Tell her about the footprints," said Jack.

"There's something big out there. I'm talking over twenty feet at least judging by the foot size."

"So some large animal killed a couple of farmers? And you come rushing in here?"

"It's not some bear or wild boar. It's larger than anything known. I think that calls for some cause of concern, yes?" said Rebecca.

"Tell her about the pictures," said Jack.

"You know I can hear you right?" said Ragazza, "What's this about pictures?"

"We, I, took pictures of the bodies and these footprints."

"Let's see 'em then," said Ragazza.

"Shouldn't we take this to the Chief?" said Rebecca.

"I'm hoping we don't need to bother him," said Ragazza.

"Well it might be better to so we don't have to go through this twice," said Jack.

"And he'd probably appreciate it knowing from the start what we're going to show you."

Ragazza led them down a hallway to a large door. She knocked and she heard a "Come in," before she opened the door.

Chief Foro was a large man. He looked like someone taught a bull how to walk and then stuffed him into a police uniform. He had more hair than the average cop, but then again he wasn't an average cop. He was the Chief of Clapham, the cricket capitol of the country. His face was bushy and his sleeves were rolled up to show off how hairy his arms were.

A bowl of dried crickets sat on his desk. They were closer to him than the chairs reserved for his guests.

"Deputy Ragazza, what brings you to my office uninvited?" said Foro.

"Well Chief, these two here said they found a couple of bodies out by the brother's farm."

"Really? You better come inside then," said Foro.

The trio walked inside and Ragazza closed the door behind them.

"What were you two doing out there? Ain't it private property?" said Foro.

"No, it's actually not private property. I was out there for my cricket experiments during the meteor shower," said Rebecca.

"And you? Mr.-?"

"Strafer. I'm writing a piece about Ms. Nove's experiment," said Jack.

"Please have a seat," said Foro.

Rebecca sat and Jack followed. Ragazza stood over them. It's unlikely she would have sat even if there were another chair for her. Rebecca grabbed for the bowl of crickets and tossed a few into her mouth.

"That things pretty cool, what did it cost?" said Foro staring at Jack.

"My arm," said Jack.

"So you found bodies? I'm glad you came to the police. We'll have to get out there and figure out who murdered these farmers."

"They weren't murdered," said Jack.

"Oh do you think it was an accident?" said Foro.

"We think something killed them. Some sort of animal. Something really big," said Jack.

"A big animal, you mean like a bear?" said Foro.

"Yeah if a bear can be twenty feet tall," said Rebecca.

"Nothing alive is that big," said Ragazza.

"There is and it's out there killing people," said Jack.

"Did you bring these people here to waste my time, deputy?" said Foro.

"Why is this so hard to believe?" said Jack.

"We didn't say we didn't believe you, but we're trying to gather all the evidence first," said Ragazza.

"I told you we have the photos," said Jack.

"Alright, let's see 'em," said Foro.

Jack looked at Rebecca and she nodded at him. He took out his phone and brought the photos up. After a series of Jim's bar photos and the crickets, came the twisted truck. It was still upside down in the photo. Preserved forever showing the damage whatever it was that did it. Foro's face shrunk as he saw the next picture. It was Karl's corpse without his head.

"What the fuck? I thought you said an animal did this?" said Ragazza.

"An animal?" said Foro, "This looks like he got drunk, took a spin in the truck and forgot to wear his seatbelt."

"Hold on, there's more," said Jack.

Ragazza gasped when the photo after showed Bill's goo filled skull.

"That looks like it's been decaying for years," said Foro.

"That's impossible. I saw Bill at Jim's a few days ago," said Ragazza.

"Is that black stuff leaking from his eye sockets. It burns and I'm guessing strips flesh like it's wax," said Rebecca.

"What about Judy?"

"We found her too," said Rebecca.

"I don't think anyone should see what happened to her," said Jack.

"Why's that Mr. Strafer?"

There came a knocking at the door. Chief Foro threw his eyes at Ragazza to answer it. An exhausted Sunshower was standing there.

"Chief, we have an outbreak. We need to close down the roads and establish a perimeter immediately," said Sunshower.

"Please come in and wait your turn, doctor," sighed Foro, "Now where were we?"

"This can't wait. People are dying and more people will die," said Sunshower.

"Alright, what is it?" said Foro.

"Hold on. We still need to show you the footprints," said Jack.

"Whatever you were showing the Chief can wait, Strafer," said Sunshower, "This is more important than a couple of photos."

"Sun, it's more than just photos," said Rebecca, "People have died."

"People have died at the hospital too. That's why I'm here. We need a quarantine."

"I'm confused as to why you came here to ask. If I'm not mistaken, I thought I told that nurse on the phone that there's no way we're doing a quarantine of an entire town," said Foro.

"Chief there won't be a town left unless we have a goddamn quarantine."

"What are you on about?"

"Chief, this disease could wipe out the entire town within days."

"You're wasting your time here doctor," said Foro.

"What kind of disease is it?" said Jack.

"It's like some sort of super leprosy," said Sunshower, "Their bodies start decaying and leaking black tar."

"Black tar?" said Jack.

"Yeah we had a patient dissolve into black goo," said Sunshower, "More like she popped."

"Does the black tar look like this?" said Jack holding up the photo of Bill's skull.

"Christ, yes. It's exactly like that," said Sunshower.

The photo showed a single footprint. It left the impression of five clawed toes.

"What do you think it is?" said Foro.

"Us? We were hoping someone here would know," said Rebecca.

"You're the scientist, aren't you?" said Foro.

"My specialty is bugs. Not megafauna. They're completely opposite. You wouldn't expect an astronaut to know about the Mariana Trench, would you?" said Rebecca.

Another knock came from the door. Foro threw his eyes at Ragazza who tossed hers at Sunshower who opened the door. The trucker, Isaac Shaw, was standing there. He looked even more exhausted than the doctor did when he knocked. He stepped into the room and looked around at the faces who were staring back at him.

"Can I help you?" said Foro.

"What are you folks doing here? Did I step into some sort of town committee?"

"It doesn't concern you Shaw. More importantly, why are you here?" said Foro.

"Considering my only friend just was killed, I figured I'd come down and tell what it was that killed him."

"Unless you're turning yourself in for the murder I don't have time for this," said Foro.

"What the Chief means is that another officer can help you," said Ragazza.

"I think the Chief will want to hear this. It wasn't any murder. Well not by a human anyway."

"Since it's everyone bothering the Chief night I'll entertain you," said Foro.

"Chief, I wouldn't be here to bother you if it weren't a giant armadillo that killed Kotto," said Shaw.

"These two tell me they found some dead farmers. The doctor is saying there some new plague. And now you're saying there's a giant armadillo killing people. There's way too many of you in my office. Who keeps letting you back here? Does no one respect a closed door anymore?" said Foro.

"Hear me out here Chief. I'm telling you there's a goddamn monster out there killing people," said Shaw.

"Fine, but this better not be some joke like the idiots and the lake sharks," said Foro.

"I'm telling you this giant armadillo-thing came out of the ground, ripped open our trucks, ate our crickets then ate Kotto. Well it drank Kotto's blood like a goddamn bottle of wine," said Shaw.

"It seems to me that you're the only one who's been drinking wine, Shaw," said Foro.

"I'm telling you this monster drank Kotto's blood and bit off his head," said Shaw.

"That's bullshit. Armadillos only eat what they dig up," said Rebecca.

"This isn't no ordinary armadillo, bug lady," said Shaw.

"What the hell I thought armadillos only ate plants," said Jack.

"Have you ever even set foot in a library?" said Rebecca.

"Hey lady I'll have you know I'm college educated and I spent plenty of time in a library," said Jack.

"Yeah? Did you actually read anything in between fucking girls between bookshelves?" said Rebecca.

"That's my business," said Jack.

"No, they eat meat. Mostly bugs, but they're not herbivores, Mr. Reporter," said Rebecca.

"I guess we look like ants to it now," said Shaw.

"You really think a twenty five foot tall armadillo attacked you then managed to get away before anyone else saw it?" said Ragazza.

"When you put it that way it sounds ridiculous," said Shaw.

"At least you know you're crazy," said Ragazza.

"I'm not crazy. I know what I saw and what I saw was a giant armadillo."

"How could there be a giant armadillo?" said Ragazza.

"Maybe it came from space," said Jack.

"You think a giant armadillo is an alien from space?" said Rebecca.

"Why not? We're dealing with something weird here. It could be anything," said Jack.

"Let's stick to the real world, Jack, not some sci-fi movie you saw when you were five," said Rebecca.

"Weren't there giant armadillos in prehistoric times?" said Sunshower.

"Now something like that is more likely. A relic from the past," said Rebecca.

"This ain't prehistoric times, this was tonight," said Shaw.

"It could be a regular armadillo that's been mutated. Who knows what effects the Perseids have on our wildlife? That's why I'm doing my study on them with the crickets," said Rebecca.

"Oh really Rebecca? You think the twenty five foot tall armadillo is mutated?" said Ragazza.

"It could be. The damn thing smelled horrible too. Maybe it was some nuclear waste I was smelling," said Shaw.

"How horrible?" said Rebecca and Sunshower together.

"A rotten stench was in the air around it," said Shaw.

Jack, Sunshower, and Rebecca looked at each other. Jack showed Shaw the footprint picture and Shaw nodded.

"Yeah I'd say that's about the right size given the claw I saw snatch Kotto," said Shaw.

"It says here that armadillos carry leprosy," said Jack.

"What?" said Sunshower.

"I'm looking on my phone it says that armadillos carry leprosy, but it usually isn't contagious to humans," said Jack.

"That actually makes some sense. A woman said the word 'armadillo' before she died tonight," said Sunshower.

"And you didn't think to bring it up until now?" said Rebecca.

"I didn't remember until this second. People say all sorts of weird things before they croak. Plus there's a lot going on, Nove," said Sunshower.

"Next time you should mention something like that sooner. But this isn't a regular armadillo we're dealing with. Who knows how contagious the leprosy it's carrying is," said Rebecca.

"If we are dealing with an armadillo; how do we stop it?" said Jack.

"Don't they have soft underbellies? Can't we just shoot the fucking thing?" said Sunshower.

"I saw its belly and it were anything, but soft," said Shaw.

"What do you mean?" said Rebecca.

"The whole thing was covered in armored plating. There weren't any soft bits on the damn thing."

The Chief slammed his fists onto to his desk. The voices in the room grew silent. Their faces turned from each other to the bull in a uniform.

"I can't believe I'm letting all of you discuss this in my office. There will be no more talk of monster armadillos until we find some real proof," said Foro.

"Chief Foro, I understand you need evidence, but isn't this extraordinary circumstances?" said Jack.

"Mr. Strafer, if we don't keep our system in chcck during the extremes we're likely to slip when it's easy," said Foro.

"What about the photos of the footprints?" said Jack.

"Mr. Strafer, those footprints could be anything. It could be a large bear or a mountain lion. Hell, someone like Shaw here could be playing an elaborate hoax on this entire town," said Foro.

"I'm not playing anything," said Shaw.

"I don't think Isaac Shaw could hoax a disease," said Sunshower.

"Maybe it's a bad case of the flu that's killing your patients, doc, but it isn't an armadillo," said Foro.

"I've never seen a flu like this before Chief."

"You want me to believe the man who's had multiple DUIs that a giant armadillo killed a man who smoked so much pot that his shit had seeds in it?" said Foro.

"I'm telling you that's what I saw," said Shaw.

"This is ridiculous. I can't shut down an entire town on a hunch. I can't call in the national guard for a giant monster when I have no proof of it," said Foro.

"Let's show you then," said Shaw.

"What?" said Foro.

"You don't believe that Kotto had his head bit off and what those folks are saying. You think I wanted my night to go this way? To see someone I cared about be ripped apart by a goddamn armadillo? Well how about we show you that we aren't full of shit," said Shaw.

"You're joking? I've got more important things to do around here," said Foro.

"It'd get us out of your office," said Jack.

"Fine, but if this is some elaborate hoax then I'm charging you all," said Foro.

"With what?" said Rebecca.

"I don't know yet, but something," said Foro.

The group audibly agreed in unison.

"Now can you all get out of my office so I have a few minutes to think about all this shit you just told me," said Foro.

The group left and headed to the front of the police station. Rebecca, Sunshower, and Ragazza led with Shaw and Jack in the rear.

"I guess I should get back to the hospital and tell them there's no quarantine coming," said Sunshower.

"It's coming, we just need to find proof," said Rebecca.

"You don't need me for that, do you?" said Sunshower.

"I have no problem with not helping, but Rebecca will be driving you back," said Ragazza.

"What? Me? Why?" said Rebecca.

"Cause I can tell you're still high," said Ragazza.

"Come on, I can drive fine high. I drive better when I'm high. Can't you cut me some slack?" said Sunshower.

"Not arresting you right now is cutting you slack, Sun. The Chief would have my ass if he knew I let you drive around high. Rebecca, you drop him off," said Ragazza.

"Hey, that's alright by me. I know you've been wanting to drive my car since I got it," said Sunshower.

Jack stood there like a pillar.

"What about me?" Jack said.

"Why don't you drive Rebecca's SUV?" said Ragazza.

"Oh I don't think that's a good idea," said Rebecca.

"Why the hell not?" said Ragazza.

"It's just that there's a lot of valuable stuff in there. I don't let anyone drive it. It's not because of your-"

"It's alright, I get it," said Jack.

"Your car is at Jim's still, right Jack?" said Ragazza.

"Yeah, it hasn't grown legs and walked I hope," said Jack.

"Fine, we'll drop you off there with Shaw and you can both ride together. Unless you have a problem with that?"

"No problem here. I appreciate it," said Jack.

"Looks like they're putting the undesirables together," said Shaw.

"You two go ahead then. Who knows how long it'll take the Chief. He's probably in the bathroom," said Ragazza.

Rebecca flung a wave and Sunshower climbed into the passenger seat of his own car. They pulled away in a hurry and their taillights were chasing after them.

## CHAPTER 8

"You don't think what I said was offensive right?" said Rebecca.

"What about Jack?" said Sunshower.

"Yeah."

"He's probably a good driver if he's been driving that piece of shit and it hasn't blown up yet."

"Yeah and like I said it was only because of my valuable equipment."

"You don't have to explain yourself to me, bug lady."

"Don't you start."

Sunshower stared out the window at the night sky as Rebecca cruised along the highway. A meteor zipped across the stars and a smile came over the doctor.

"So how do you like it?" he said.

"It drives pretty damn nice. I'm a little jealous," she said.

"It's what you can afford when you decide to study people instead of bugs," he said.

"You really believe that trucker guy?"

"What that there's a giant armadillo running around killing people and spreading a disease that makes people pop into goo?" he said.

"He didn't say that second part," she said.

"Yeah, but you did."

"True. Well, do you really believe all of it?"

"I guess so."

"What if the Chief is right and it is some new plague? You saw the footprints," she said.

"Maybe it's a large bear or a hoax. Shaw's nice for a drinking buddy and all, but I'm not sure he's all there."

"Do you think your patients will be alright?"

"It's hard to know. Hopefully the leprosy treatments work."

"And when you say a patient popped into goo?"

"It was like stepping on a bloated tick."

"I think you should do the midnight doctor,"

"I already gave my speech for the night."

"And that's never stopped you before from doing more than one."

"You hate the midnight doctor," he said.

"Yeah, I do, but it could help save lives if you tell people to stay inside."

"Shouldn't we tell them to leave town?"

"What about both?"

Sunshower took out his phone and held it out in front of himself.

"Hey there folks, it's your favorite late night prep talker, the midnight doctor. Today's not only a double dose day, but it's also a very important message. I know I have fans all over the world and I love all my night patients, but this is message for those a little more local. Anyone who lives in Clapham like me should stay inside tonight. There's a real nasty bug going around and it's not something you want to catch. Trust me on this one folks, stay out from public places and take the time to get to know your lovers a little better. And to those without lovers or uninterested in that sort of thing, catch up on a TV show or podcast."

"Don't forget about the leave town," said Rebecca.

"Thanks special assistant Rebecca. Yes, if you want to leave town and have a safe place to go then please make a swift evacuation. Alright, that's it. I'll see you all tomorrow night. Be safe out there."

"Hey Sun, I think Shaw's right about the armadillo," she said.

"What makes you say- oh," he said.

The Armordillo was crossing the road. It was taking its time despite its size. It could easily cross in a few steps, but it stood there in the middle of the road. Rebecca slowed to a crawl in the mustang and kept her foot on the brake. She dimmed her lights, but the Armordillo could still be seen from the lamp posts. There was only about thirty feet between the car and the beast.

"Jesus, fuck, it's gigantic," he said.

"What were you expecting?" she said.

"I didn't think we'd actually run across it. I was hoping not to which is why I was going back to the hospital in the first place," he said.

"What do you think it wants?" he said.

"Food probably. I doubt it has any evil intentions beyond stuffing its face," she said.

"Yeah, but we can't let it go around eating us," he said.

"Of course not. And if it gets to town it'll tear through our factories within a day."

"Alright then we've got to stop in," he said.

"I knew you'd come around," she said.

"I should probably get some footage right?" he said.

"I mean, yes, but also no since we're dealing with a huge beast here that's already killed a bunch of people."

"Oh good, for a second I thought you'd want me to go out there and get some evidence for the Chief so help would arrive sooner," he said.

Rebecca's fingers strummed the wheel and she looked down before locking eyes with him.

"Well we do need evidence or the Chief won't call backup."

"Come on, you can't be serious," he said.

"It was your idea," she said.

"I was only trying to sound heroic."

"Why not try the real thing?"

"I don't know, Shaw said that thing ripped off Kotto's head."

"It would boost your followers," she said, "When you share the footage later of course. Everyone will want to follow Doctor Midnight, the man who took on the Armordillo."

"Armordillo?"

"The creature needs a name doesn't it?"

"We'll decide on that later. But not that, that's horrible. I get a veto if I'm going out there."

Sunshower reached into his pockets for a gorilla biscuit, but there were none left. He had taken the last one earlier and his backup was in the pocket of Jack Strafer. He had his hand on the door handle and took a deep breathe.

"This is dumb right?"

"Incredibly."

"Only making sure. Alright, fine. Keep the car running and I'll be right back."

"You don't want me to come with you?"

"Now you want this to be a team effort?"

"Not really."

"Just keep the goddamn car running."

Rebecca watched as he slowly snuck up on the Armordillo with his phone held out to record it as he went. He didn't make a sound. He didn't yell to get the creature's attention. The Armordillo was looked as if it were resting in the road. One might confuse it for sunbathing if the sun had been out. Instead it large eyes were looking up to the sky and watching the meteors fall.

Sunshower snapped a photo and the camera shutter sound went off.

The Armordillo's big nostrils flared and its eyes turned from the skies to the road it was on. Sunshower had been spotted. He tossed a glance back at Rebecca and slowly walked backwards to the car. The Armordillo's tongue shot out to taste the air as it charged towards Sunshower running on all fours. He slammed the door as the Armordillo gained ground. Rebecca shifted into reverse and Sunshower screamed at the creature who was only a few feet away.

"Get us the fuck out of here," he yelled.

"I'm trying," she said.

The car zipped backwards and the Armordillo chased after it. It eyes were shining in the headlights while it pursued its prey. The cars wheels revved faster with Rebecca's eyes locked on the rear view mirror to see where she's going. It was mostly straight out in these plains, but occasionally a bend would occur. Unfortunately there was one ahead, or behind them now.

"There's a turn coming up," she said.

"Make it!"

She spun the wheel around the best she could, but then the car stopped moving. Rebecca's eyes slowly shifted from the mirror down to the windshield in front of her. A claw was sticking down through the hood of the car.

"What happened? I mean, I see the fucking claw, but what happened?"

"I think it killed your engine."

The scientist and the doctor saw the Armordillo's face nearly beaming back at them as it removed its claw from the mustang.

"What do we do now?"

"It's gonna kill us. It's gonna fuckin' kill us. And eat us," said Rebecca.

"I say we make a run for it," said Sunshower.

"Run where? There's nothing out here," she said.

The Armordillo let out a roar that almost shattered their eardrums. It's mouth opened and they could see the monster's razor sharp teeth that lined inside.

RAAAARURRUNG!

Sunshower opened his door and the large eyes darted on him. He ran towards the right and the Armordillo took off after him. Rebecca stepped out a moment later towards the left.

She could feel the vibrations in the earth as the Armordillo pursued Sunshower. She didn't know how long she was running for. She eventually decided to circle back a little when she felt the ground calm. There were fire-barrel cacti around her when she heard something once more.

Sunshower's voice called to her in a whisper. He was ducked behind a large rock. Rebecca made her way over with no sign of the Armordillo following her.

"Are you alright?" she said.

"Yeah, you?"

"I'm okay."

"We've got to hold out until help comes. They should be here any minute. They've got to come down this way," said Sunshower.

They could hear the horrible scream of the Armordillo once more throughout the night.

"It knows we're out here," she said.

"Well it knows I'm out here."

"What are you talking about? It saw me leave the car too."

"Did it? It's head turned to watch me, I'm not sure it knows you're here."

"So what?"

"So I'm going to give it what it wants."

"Are you insane?"

"Would you rather us both die?"

"Neither of us have to die. I don't think this thing, this armadillo, doesn't pick out targets."

"You're a scientist right?"

"Yeah."

"Let me test that hypothesis."

"That doesn't make any sense!"

Sunshower stood up and started to walk away without a word.

"Now's not the time to be heroic," said Rebecca after him.

He continued walking in silence. She quietly followed behind and they were soon back overlooking the car.

The Armordillo was pacing around the destroyed mustang. It's claws played with it like it were a Matchbox car. It poked a tire and it popped with a bang. The Armordillo bent down and chew the rubber, but spit it out soon after. It's claw then sliced through the roof and the car was split apart.

Sunshower slowly made his descent towards the beast. He threw up a stopping hand back towards Rebecca. She went back up the hill and crouched down into a prone position.

He held his phone up to snap a few more seconds of video. *The Chief will have to believe this.* The Armordillo was tossing pieces of metal like it were paper. Sunshower scuttled down the hill and roared at the beast.

"You want me? Come and get me," he yelled.

The sludge covered him a moment later. It poured out from the wrists of the claws. His legs were pinned to the ground, but he still stood upright. His phone still recording all the way. The beast made its way towards the stuck doctor with slow deliberate steps. The Armordillo whipped its tail around in the air, breaking the sound barrier as it did so. The spear-like tip slashed around high before plunging right through Sunshower's chest from behind. Sunshower looked at Rebecca with tears in his eyes before the tail sliced upward. His phone falling into the goo and his body being torn in half vertically. His entrails fell to the Chihuahuan Desert's sand. The Armordillo's face was covered in Sunshower's blood. There was no scream.

The Armordillo glanced towards Rebecca, its tongue licking its mouth and face clean, before letting out another roar. It moved faster up the hill towards Rebecca. She jumped from the prone position to her feet and booked it.

*That fucking idiot died for nothing. It knew I was here the whole time.*

There was a moment of silence and Rebecca turned around. The creature was shifting. Rebecca watched as the Armordillo curled itself into a large ball. Its limbs folded onto themselves. Its tailed curled inside itself and disappeared. She couldn't tell where the ball began and where it ended. It was one continuous smooth armor plated rolling wrecking ball.

The monstrous bowling ball was headed in her direction. She took off back into the desert. Past the rocks. Past the cacti. She could hear the sand and stones flying through the air as the monster chased her.

*A cricket truck must have disposed some of its pallets here, Goddamn littering morons. These idiots think this desert is their personal dump.* She ran towards the pile and dug a spot out in it. The Armordillo ball rolled by and she managed to catch her breath. She could see the Armordillo rolling off into the night through cracks in the pile.

*I've got to hold out. Sunshower was right. Help is coming. Ragazza and the Chief. That guy with the arm and the trucker. They'll be here. I know it.*

## CHAPTER 9

Jack was cruising in his Ford Pinto with Shaw in the passenger seat. They had been dropped off and now following the police cruiser that held Deputy Ragazza and Chief Foro. Jack had told them to follow him, but they decided not to follow that instruction. They were headed out through the desert to the farmlands.

"It's a little quiet in here, mind if I turn on the radio?" said Shaw.

Shaw pushed the console button, but it didn't work.

"You're telling me this car doesn't even have a working radio? How am I going to get pumped up to fight this thing?"

"Check the glove compartment," said Jack.

Shaw opened the glove compartment revealing a pocket radio amongst the papers inside. He grabbed it, extended the antenna and flicked it on. Jazz music came out. Shaw moved the tuner around and only static came through. He moved it back to the jazz station and held it.

"Yeah it only gets that one station. No matter where I go," said Jack.

"Are you fucking kidding me?" said Shaw.

"Well, alright, it also gets the weather band."

"You feel safe driving this thing?" said Shaw.

"Why wouldn't I?" said Jack.

"Cause you don't even have a fucking radio," said Shaw looking around, "So you're a journalist right? Do you normally cover giant monsters?"

"Nah usually sports."

"Awesome. I'd love to get paid to watch sports and write about them. That must be the best job ever."

"It's something."

"I bet you're mad they sent you here to cover a stupid story about meteors."

"At least it's turning into a monster movie."

"Yeah. I'm still a little in disbelief myself over seeing the fucker. What was the last game you went to?"

"I was covering a little league baseball championship."

"Oh. Wow. Man. Kids playing ball is always a sight. They still give it their all. Man. That must really be the life. You're lucky."

"I guess so. Sorry to hear about your friend by the way."

"He is a good man. Unfortunately not the brightest. I apologize if he said anything to offend you at the bar. He's not good at being friendly. I suppose I should start saying 'wasn't.'"

"I've had my share of ribbing."

"So you been living in your car or just while you're in town?"

"Little of both. Journalism doesn't exactly pay big money."

"Well if you ever wanted to ship crickets, I could get you in."

"I'll keep that in mind, thanks."

A meteor zipped across the sky and Jack let out a smile.

"Yeah it never gets old seeing those thing fly. Most people out here take them for granted and I guess I do too sometimes, but it's nice when you stop and look at them," said Shaw.

"I wonder where they come from," said Jack.

"From space."

"Yes, but from how far away? From the asteroid belt or from somewhere further? You ever think something from way outside our galaxy ever lands here?"

"I'm sure that's happened, but it doesn't matter much whether it did or not."

"Why not?"

"It just doesn't, Jack."

"I thought you had some theory about diseases from outer space?"

"That was Kotto."

Ragazza stared at the road ahead of her. The Chief was riding shotgun and staring out the window.

"They're really zipping out there," he said.

"What are?" she said.

"The meteors. I've never seen them so active."

"Yeah they seems to be more of them than usual this year. What do you think is going on around here Chief?"

"I don't know Ragazza. I've never heard of a giant armadillo, but I'd never heard of many things before they happen."

"So you think it's possible?"

"Anything is possible, but you can't expect me to call in the military over something we can't prove."

"We've had multiple witnesses."

"And none of them cops. It's not like you saw it. That'd be different. A doctor who's high, a scientist bugged out of her mind, an out of towner journalist, and insane trucker saw a giant armadillo. It could be one of those shared hallucinations."

"And if it isn't?"

"Then we kill the fucker. Preferable by ourselves. This is a nice town. I don't want a whole bunch of tourists flooding here to see where the giant armadillo was."

"That'd be great for business."

"I don't care, it'd be humiliating."

"Is that what this is about? You don't want to get help because you think it's embarrassing?"

"Little of both, we still need proof. Who's going to listen to us if we don't have hard evidence?"

"You keep going on about this proof-"

"Deputy, brakes!"

Ragazza slammed on the brakes. She nearly slammed right into the wreckage that was once Sunshower's new mustang. The car could barely be identified as once being a mustang, but the police knew the color and the police knew Sunshower drove it.

"Oh god, do you think?" said Ragazza.

"Get out slowly and keep your gun drawn," said Foro.

"Yes, Chief," said Ragazza.

"And one more thing," said Foro.

"Yeah, Chief?"

"Don't forget the shotgun. Also, be careful."

Ragazza grabbed the shotgun and holstered it to her back. They got out with their pistols in the air and headed to the wreckage.

The Ford Pinto also parked with Shaw and Jack climbing out walking behind the police.

The four covered their mouths as they got closer to the scene. Not only in precaution of what they might see, but the smell of dead lingered about.

Bits of flesh and intestine covered the road. A head torn in two laid near each other by the sparse grass on the side. One half was melted by the black tar. It was practically a dollar store skull while the other had loose skin dangling down with an eyeball to match.

"Holy fuck, what happened here?" said Ragazza.

"Language, Deputy," said Foro.

"The goddamn Armordillo came and sliced Sunshower in half. I managed to run away and I think I lost it for now. I saw your lights and here I am," said Rebecca.

She had crept out from the shadows.

"Rebecca? Are you alright?" said Ragazza.

"I'm fine, but how many people have to die until we call in some help?" she said.

"I'm all about getting help once we know what we're dealing with," said Foro.

"We've known what we're dealing with!"

"I need to see it for myself. I need some real proof," said Foro.

"Proof? You want more proof? I told you it killed Sunshower. For Christ's sake his body is right there."

"What we have is a dead body. Not proof of a giant armadillo running around."

"Fine then check his phone."

"Pardon?"

"Sunshower was recording footage before he died. Look at his phone."

"Sure, where is it?"

"It's in the goo."

"Lot of good it'll do us in there."

"We need to take it out."

"Doesn't that stuff melt your skin?"

"Yes, but someone will have to grab it anyway."

"Listen, lady, I've had it up to here with this shit. I'm not going to burn my flesh because of a joke."

"So you believe the goo melts you, but not that an armadillo sprayed it?"

"I'm not taking the chance."

"Fine I'll do it," said Jack, "I know you're all waiting for me to volunteer. The man with a fake hand to grab the phone.

Fine. Who cares if it melts? It's not like it was a ton of money and still a crappy model anyway."

"Jack you don't have to-" said Shaw.

"No one else will," said Jack.

"It smells fucking wretched," said Ragazza.

"Be happy you're not the one about to touch it then," said Jack.

Jack scrunched his nose as he approached the goo. A big bubble formed and popped as he plunged his prosthetic arm into the sludge pile that was once Sunshower. The hand couldn't feel in the traditional sense. He had to rely on his upper arm to feel something clang against the prosthetic. Some bile escaped from Jack's mouth as he pulled out the phone with a rotting hand still attached. Jack wiggled the phone and the hand dropped to the floor with a plop, splattering it into oblivion. The phone itself didn't look much better. It had the benefit of being metal and plastic, but it was already heavily eroded. Even if the battery still worked it wouldn't matter; the screen was gone.

Jack's hand suffered a similar fate. The bits melted together and when he flexed his arm, the hand didn't open or close anymore. It was stuck in a melted form.

Jack walked back and the group gathered around. Ragazza brought a cloth from the cruiser and wiped the phone off.

"Well that's great. What a waste that was," said Foro.

"The SD card might still be good," said Jack.

"Alright, let's check it," said Ragazza.

Ragazza popped the card out from the side and held it up. It didn't appear damaged at all.

"We'll use Jack's phone, it's only right he keeps the card," said Rebecca.

"That card is evidence and property of the police," said Foro.

"Fine, but for now we'll play it on Jack's phone at least," said Rebecca.

Jack stood staring down at his rotting prosthetic arm.

"There something wrong?" said Shaw.

"You think you could help me with-"

"Hey, yeah, no problem," said Shaw.

Shaw reached under the back of Jack's shirt and loosened the prosthetic. The arm dropped to the ground and the hand shattered. Shaw looked at it then Jack who shrugged.

"It's alright, even if I got a hand replacement the stench would have never gone away," said Jack.

Jack reached into his pocket and pulled out his own phone. He placed it in the armpit of his missing arm and took the SD card from Ragazza. He slipped the card in and took the phone back into his hand. The files were intact. The group grew tighter to watch Sunshower's recording. The Armordillo was clearly there. It was mad as hell and destroying the mustang that laid before them. The last seconds of footage were of the sludge pouring from the Armordillo onto Sunshower with the tail slice coming thereafter.

The Chief was silent. Jack slipped the phone back into the pocket and Rebecca broke the silence.

"Is that proof enough for you?" said Rebecca.

"It is," he said.

"Well Chief, how are we going to stop this Armordillo?" said Rebecca.

"Armordillo?" said Jack.

"Who came up with that stupid name?" said Shaw.

"It's what Sunshower was calling it before he died. I'm thinking we should keep that name in his honor," said Rebecca.

"Alright I guess it's what we'll call it," said Shaw.

"I don't know. I don't think it really needs a name," said Jack.

"I thought you were a writer. Shouldn't you come up with a name to help branding?" said Shaw.

"Yeah, but that's for the people to decide," said Jack.

"Sunshower was a person and he decided," said Rebecca.

"Now's not the time for this," said Ragazza.

"Alright. Let's get back to more important things. Chief, now that you believe it exists, what are you going to do about it?" said Rebecca.

"I'm going to shoot the damn thing," said Foro.

"What?" said Rebecca.

"There's nothing my gun can't take care of," said Foro.

"What about back up and a quarantine?" said Rebecca.

"I don't need backup to get rid of this thing. I can do it myself and we won't need to worry about the leprosy spreading," said Foro.

They could hear the rocks kicking up and hitting the ground. It sounded like rain on a tin roof. The Armordillo had returned. It was still curled into a ball. It rolled from the side of the road right onto the police cruiser. The car was flattened like it had been run over by a steamroller.

"Here's your chance, Chief," said Jack, "You better hope you're right."

"How the hell does that thing move so fast?" said Ragazza.

"Get back! Get to cover!" said Foro.

The group ran to the hilled area Rebecca was hiding to watch the Chief take down the beast. The ball had now come to a stop. It uncurled itself and the Armordillo had its sharp teeth on display. Its tail swung through the air with its little sonic booms rattling through the air with each sway.

Chief Foro aimed his pistol at the snarling beast. He fired three rounds directly into the chest of the monster. The group saw they were all direct hits. But there was something wrong. The creature still stood. The Armordillo let out a soft roar. Almost as if it were laughing at the cop. It stood as if nothing had even touched it.

"Now what?" said Shaw.

The Armordillo sliced a claw at Foro who rolled out of the way. He shot another round at the claw and it too bounced off as if it were nothing. The rest of his magazine did the same. The bullets sparked off into the road. The Armordillo charged at him.

Foro turned his head back towards Ragazza.

"Call backup, call any-" he said as the sludge covered him.

A pile of black tar melted where once stood a bull in a uniform. And before they knew it, the Armordillo dove back into the solid ground as if it were a pool of water. Dirt and rocks went flying through the air. It swam through the ground with great ease. Rocks, debris, and fossils were turned to sand. The Armordillo was the immovable force and there were no rock to contain it. That may be because the immovable rock was adjoined to the body of the creature. It was covered in armored plating after all.

"Chief!" yelled Ragazza.

She ran towards the sludge pile and Shaw grabbed her from embracing it.

"He may have been a bit of a dick, but-"said Ragazza.

"I know," said Shaw.

"He didn't seem that bad to me. Journalists require sources, police require evidence," said Jack.

"Course now you say, now that he's dead," said Ragazza.

"I recall saying it earlier too," said Jack.

"Do we have to argue about this right now? We tried to warn the Chief. He had to find out for himself the hard way. We have more pressing issues. For instance, what about the Armordillo? Where is it going?" said Rebecca.

"Why did it even leave? Is it playing games with us?" said Shaw.

"It might be after a bigger fish," said Jack.

"It might be about quantity," said Ragazza.

"Sunshower thought it might be headed to the cricket factory," said Rebecca.

"That'd make sense. That thing can eat. It devoured both Kotto and my truck's cargo and it still wants more," said Shaw.

"Doesn't make much sense to me. The thing seems to be wandering around out here," said Jack, "There's very little indication that it's headed anywhere."

"I'm the scientist here, Jack," said Rebecca, "It's headed to town."

"Alright gang, enough chatter. Tie your shoes. We have to go after it," said Ragazza.

"On foot? Are you nuts?" said Rebecca.

"The cruiser's been destroyed," said Ragazza.

"Fuck, on foot it is," said Rebecca.

"We still have my car," said Jack.

Ragazza and Rebecca tossed glances back at each other.

"Oh right, how could we forget?" said Rebecca.

"Come on, let's get after it," said Shaw headed back to Pinto.

Jack headed for the driver's door and Rebecca stopped him after he opened it.

"Are you sure you don't want someone else to drive?"

"Nah, I'm good. It's my car after all. I wouldn't want someone else to drive it. No offense or anything, there's just some valuable things in here," he said before sitting down in the seat.

"You're going to let him drive?" said Rebecca.

"It's his car," said Ragazza.

"Can't you commandeer it or something?"

"Yeah, that doesn't happen as much as you think."

Jack realized his mistake and got back out of the car. He then pulled the front seat back forward to let Rebecca and Ragazza into the back. Shaw was already snug in the passenger seat. Ragazza cozied up behind him, tossing clothes and papers onto the floor beneath her.

"Sorry about the mess," said Jack.

"It's fine," said Ragazza, "But can we be quiet for a few minutes while I radio in some help?"

That'd be easy enough. Shaw was passed out before she finished talking while Rebecca closed her eyes thinking of a nice beach far away.

Jack got back into the driver's seat and revved off towards the town. The meteors continued to fall during the summer night. They had fallen this time each year, but this year was different. This year was when the meteors woke up the Armordillo. It stretched his four limbs out and began the walk towards the main town of Clapham. It wouldn't take long to get there. It would take even less time to eat every last cricket in the factory.

CHAPTER 10

The call rang through the night. Sunshower's last recorded message coupled with online bulletins and radio messages were broad-casted telling citizens in town to find shelter on the outskirts. The night owls woke up their family members and ushered them to safety. The official message was a tornado was headed to town out of nowhere. This coupled with a bad flu was news enough to spread and get people to safety. There was a high school on the edge of town where people were told to gather if they had no where else to go.

Cars poured out of the center of Clapham as the Ford Pinto drove in. Jack had the wheel with Shaw slowly waking up and Ragazza with Rebecca in the back seat. The town was your normal grid setup with apartment buildings, townhouses, and large offices sprinkled on blocks.

"It looks like its working," said Shaw.

"It's not exactly a quarantine, but its good that people are seeking help. It'll be less potential for causalities when the Armordillo shows up."

"Not everyone is going," said Rebecca.

"Yeah I see some lights still on in houses."

"People will stay," said Rebecca.

"Some people always stay," said Jack.

The Pinto continued cruising through town and there were less house lights still on.

"It ain't many. I can tell you that. I've never seen this place so empty. We can actually park wherever the hell we want. What did you tell them to send out, Ragazza?" said Shaw.

"Only that a tornado was coming. That and there's a new flu that the tornado might be carrying," she said.

"And people bought that?" said Shaw.

"Looks like they did," she said.

"The streets seem pretty empty. Maybe people actually listened for once," said Shaw.

"Or they're cowering in their basements," said Jack.

"I just hope that we're right," said Rebecca, "What if the Armordillo wasn't heading this way?"

Shaw pointed Jack towards the factory and Jack slammed on the brakes.

"I don't think we need to worry about us being right," he said.

Rebecca poked her head between the front seats and peered through the windshield. The world was split and a fresh hole was formed. It was already here.

The factory was six stories tall and houses billions of crickets. Some were alive, others frozen, and many packed with spices ready to ship out.

Jack parked the car near the hole and they all stepped out.

"What do we do?" said Jack.

"The military should be here soon to help," said Ragazza, "I guess we need to try and hold it off until then."

"Hold it off how?" said Jack.

Ragazza unholstered her pistol and held it out.

"You ever use a gun before Jack?" said Ragazza.

"No," said Jack.

"You Rebecca?"

"No," she said.

"It's all yours then Shaw," said Ragazza.

"I've never used a gun either, ma'am," he said.

"For fuck's sake, you're telling me that you're all in Texas and none of you know how to use guns?" said Ragazza.

"Look, I can take it, but I don't think I'll be that great of a shot," said Rebecca.

"That'll do, this thing is big enough that I doubt you'd miss," said Ragazza.

Ragazza handed the pistol to Rebecca who grasped it limply.

"Just flick this off and gently squeeze the trigger. And don't put your finger on the trigger unless you intend on pulling it. Running around with your finger there will only end badly for everyone here," said Ragazza, "You got it?"

"I got it," said Rebecca.

Ragazza took the shotgun off her back and cocked it dramatically.

"I've always wanted to do that," she said, "Now let's hunt this fucker."

"Where the hell is it?" said Shaw.

"It's pretty hard to lose a giant armadillo," said Rebecca.

A cry was heard through the night. An old woman could be seen a moment later running down the street past a grocery store in a night gown screaming her head off. The Armordillo was running behind her and let out a roar of its own. The Armordillo and its prey were moving away from the group of self imposed monster hunters. Sludge spewed out from its claws melting the roof of the grocery store.

"Guess we found it," said Ragazza.

"See I told you someone always stays behind," said Jack.

"We have to do something," said Shaw.

"She had her chance to get out of here," said Rebecca.

"Does she look like the type to be on the snapchat or up all night on the radio?" said Shaw.

"What do you think we're supposed to do? It's getting further and further away," said Rebecca.

"Shoot the damn thing," said Shaw.

"I can't make that shot. It's too far off," said Rebecca.

The old woman fell to the ground with the Armordillo only a few feet from her.

"Ragazza?" said Shaw.

"Give me a second to think for God's sake," she said.

"In a second that thing is going to eat her and then us," said Jack.

Jack opened his car door and climbed back inside.

"Running away already Jack?" said Rebecca, "Some journalist you are."

"You're the one that didn't want to help," said Shaw.

"At least I'm not leaving like some coward."

Jack slammed his one hand down on the car horn. Its sounded blurted through the air and the others covered their ears. The Armordillo cocked its head away from the old woman and changed its direction towards the group. It let out a roar and it's jaws snapped at the empty air above it.

"I knew these things were getting big, but sheesh," the old woman screamed.

"Lady, get the hell out of here. Get to the high school or back inside, anywhere, but the damn streets," shouted Ragazza.

The old woman took off into dark and was out of sight within seconds.

"I've never seen a geriatric move so fast, have you?" said Shaw.

Jack returned to the group with a smile.

"Maybe when there's chocolate pudding for dessert," said Jack.

The ground shook and they looked to see the Armordillo stampeding at the factory. Its claws slashed through the brick wall and it was already feasting on the vats of crickets within. It emerged a few moments later and looked upward at the factory. Jack had his phone out and was already snapping pictures and bits of video.

The Armordillo stuck a claw into the brick wall on the outside. It pushed itself upward and was climbing to the second floor. It past the second and went right past the third to the fourth.

"Rebecca you've got to take the shot," said Ragazza.

"Why me?" she said.

"This shotgun won't reach it from here," said Ragazza.

"Alright, fine," said Rebecca.

Rebecca took aim and fired the pistol. It hit a glass pane which shattered. The Armordillo didn't even notice. It continued to stuff its face filled to the brim with claws full with crickets. They cried out into the night. A billion cricket chorus screaming and singing at the panic around them.

Rebecca shot the pistol another time and this one hit. It went right into one of the armored bands on its back. The Armordillo paid notice and turned its head. Rebecca fired another three shots into the bands and they ricocheted off into the night.

It let out one of its roars and rolled down the factory. The wall of the factory broke apart as the Armordillo came crashing down into the road. Rebecca fired as it came closer to them. Each bullet doing less damage than the one before. It uncurled and stood on its hind legs. It walked towards the Pinto before stopping mid-step. It sniffed the air, and turned towards the bay that was filled with boxed crickets. Its claw ripped through the metal grating and they could hear pieces of metal clanking as it ate.

"What exactly is the plan here? Those bullets don't seem to be doing anything. Which we already knew when Foro got himself killed trying to shoot the damn thing," said Jack.

"We need to buy some time," said Ragazza.

"Buy some time? Buy some fucking time until when?" said Jack.

"I don't know Jack. Until we get some backup. Until the army comes rolling in. Or the air force drops some bombs. I just know we should try and keep it around the factory until some fucking help arrives," said Ragazza.

The radio around Ragazza's belt began to chime. She pulled it off and voice came through. It was the cop from the department. The bored one. Ragazza smiled to the group.

"See that's probably help right now," she said raising the radio up.

"Bad news, deputy," he said.

"What's that?" she said.

"The military won't be making it for another six hours," he said.

"Six hours? The base is right fucking there, it's an hour trip leisurely," she said.

"I know, but they said something about precaution and told me to get into a hazmat suit.

"Oh come on, I don't think its that bad," she said.

"You're the one who called for a quarantine. Be lucky they aren't going to nuke Clapham," he said.

"He's got to be joking, right? They wouldn't do that, right?" said Jack, "We're all feeling fine, right?"

Rebecca leaned up on the car and it took the brunt of her weight. Ragazza turned off the radio and walked over to her.

"I'm not feeling so well," she said.

"What's wrong?" said Jack.

"I don't know, I just feel numb. I can't stand," she said.

Jack walked over and she pulled up one of her sleeves. Black boils were littered about in no specific pattern on her forearm.

"Christ, you're infected," said Jack.

"You say that like I'm going to be undead," she said.

"No, just regular dead," said Jack.

"I must have somehow caught it from Sunshower," she said.

"Was he showing symptoms?"

"No, but he could have still been a carrier either way."

"Shaw, take my gun," said Rebecca.

Shaw took the pistol and held it at his side.

"I don't mean to be a downer, but what the fuck are we going to do?" said Jack.

"It doesn't seem that interested in us," said Ragazza.

"Yeah for the moment, but it will once its done eating the entire factory," said Jack.

"Plus we need to get Rebecca to the hospital," said Shaw.

"Let's the lay the facts as they are. We have no backup. We have two guns and we have an infected person among us," said Jack.

"That sounds about right," said Shaw.

"We need a plan. We need to come up with a way to stop or stall that thing while we wait," said Jack.

"I don't think Rebecca can wait," said Shaw.

"I know that, Christ, why do you keep bringing it up?" said Jack.

"Because-" said Shaw.

Jack looked to see Rebecca slumped on the ground. She wasn't dead, but merely passed out.

"Mixture of the all-nighter and leprosy I imagine," said Ragazza, "She'll be alright."

"I wish I had that optimism," said Jack, "What's the plan, deputy? These guns barely scratch that monster's armor."

"But it does notice it when we make contact," said Shaw.

"How's that going to help us?" said Jack.

"I'm not sure yet, but-"

"I know how," said Ragazza, "Shaw and I will shoot that thing while you take Rebecca to the hospital."

"You want me to leave you two alone with a giant armadillo?"

"With an Armordillo, yes," said Ragazza.

"The answer's no," said Jack.

"No?"

"No. I reject this plan. I think it's a bad one. I don't think I'm going to do it," said Jack.

"Just do the damn plan, Jack. You don't want Rebecca to die, do you?" said Shaw.

"I don't want you two to die either," said Jack.

"That's nice and all, but the Armordillo is losing interest in the factory quick," said Ragazza, "How about you get a move on, Mr. Strafer?"

It was true. The Armordillo was climbing out from the wall rubble. It was slowly walking on all fours towards the group. Fire burned brighter in its eyes with every step it took.

"Get in that shitty deathtrap of a car and take Rebecca to a hospital," said Ragazza.

Shaw was already lifting Rebecca into the Ford Pinto while Jack slowly climbed into the driver's seat.

"When do I go?" said Jack.

"You'll know," said Ragazza unhooking her radio and slipping it into Jack's pocket, "Take this and go."

Jack pressed on the gas as Ragazza and Shaw split apart. Ragazza fired her shotgun at the beast. It swiveled its head to her and started stampeding. Shaw fired the pistol from a distance away at the Armordillo's back. The Armordillo paused, it looked around then rolled towards Shaw. It was only a few feet from flattening him when Ragazza shot again. The Armordillo uncurled and roared into the air. The sun was beginning to rise over the town of Clapham. The Armordillo curled and rolled through a building. It was a pharmacy and after the Armordillo got through with it, it was a pile of nothing. It uncurled and walked towards Ragazza. Its claws slashed at the ground beneath it sending pieces of road flying towards the deputy. She jumped and ducked between the flying asphalt and fired another shot at the beast. It rose on its hind legs and ran at Ragazza. She fired again and the buck went everywhere. Shaw shot his pistol at its back, but it didn't budge. Shaw could see Ragazza and she screamed.

"Hide, Shaw, hide."

Ragazza shot once more at the head of the Armordillo before it picked her up. She lifted her shotgun in mid-air and fired at its arm. The Armordillo shook her free of the gun. Its other claw rose and each claw grabbed a different half. Its left hand had her arms and its right had her legs. The Armordillo lifted her wiggling body up and held it above its open mouth. Her eyes did not burst and she did not scream. It was over in a second. She was torn apart at the torso. Her intestines fell right into its mouth and It tossed aside the rest. It sniffed the air before diving under the ground. Its claws sliced through the concrete as if it were made of paper.

Jack with a sleeping Rebecca was speeding down the highway when he felt a rumbling underneath the ground. He slammed on the brakes and the hole formed in front of him. The Armordillo burst out and roared towards the car. Jack drove around it as fast as possible and the Armordillo curled up after it. Jack lead footed down the road. He glanced back in his mirror and the ball was on his tail. He drove even faster and glanced back again to see the Armordillo was nowhere in sight. It had vanished completely. But then the rumbling began again and he slammed on his brakes. A tear in the world had popped out of the ground nearly beneath them and the car dangled on the edge of the hole. The creature still wasn't seen.

"Fuck, what are we going to do now?" said Jack.

Rebecca lay motionless. Jack opened his door and pulled her across the seats. He lifted her between his half arm and good arm. He slung her over his back, fireman style and ran off to the side of the road. Jack could hear the roar and the Armadillo made its reappearance. It came from the hole where the Pinto was on the edge of. The beast jumped out and lifted the car up to its mouth. It held it taillights first and its jaw unhinged showing its razor sharp teeth. The jaw chomped down on the car and it exploded. The car that is. Fire flew out with metal shrapnel hitting the ground. The Pinto had blown up. Smoke filled the air and Jack covered his mouth with his shirt and Rebecca's with his hand.

The smoke cleared and the Armordillo laid on the ground. Its lower jaw was gone with blood trickling throughout the street. It was a small river you could hear the trickling sound as it flowed. The beast was dead.

"What the fuck? The people who sold my parents that car said they got that fixed," said Jack to a passed out Rebecca beside him.

Jack took the radio out from his pocket and flicked it on.

"The Armordillo is dead," he said.

"How?" the radio responded.

"Not even an Armordillo can survive an explosion in the mouth," said Jack.

"That's good, that's real good, but can I ask who's talking?" the radio said.

"I'm Jack Strafer, a reporter."

"Where's the deputy? How did you get this radio?"

"She gave it to me. I don't know where she is, but I need an ambulance. I have a woman here and she needs to get to a hospital. We're right outside town. You can't miss us. The smoke's still billowing."

"Alright Mr. Strafer. Stay calm if you can. An ambulance will be right there," the radio said.

*Stay calm? They want me to stay calm? I thought I sounded pretty damn calm. And why shouldn't I be upset anyway? How the hell can I stay calm when I lost my arm and now my car. Fuck and my laptop was in there! I really need to call my editor. Damn, maybe I do need to calm down some.*

Jack rustled through his pocket and pulled out the gorilla biscuit. He unraveled the hard candy and stared at the cricket inside it. He didn't give it a second thought before plopping it into his mouth. It was nearly dawn now and he could hear the sirens coming from a distance. He decided to close his own eyes and rest.

## CHAPTER 11

Jack woke up to find himself in a hospital bed. He glanced around the room and saw Shaw sitting in a chair in the corner. He scrunched up to sit in the bed and cleared his throat. Shaw opened his eyes and laughed.

"Looks like you finally decided to wake up," said Shaw.

"How long was I out for?" said Jack.

"Not long, only twelve hours give or take."

"Jesus, am I alright? I feel fine."

"That's cause you are fine, you were just tired is all. You collapsed from exhaustion. That's what the nurse told me anyway. I suppose killing a giant armadillo will do that to you. And you're the one that slayed it after all."

"What'd you wait for me all day?"

"What else am I going to do? My truck's been destroyed. My employer's main building has been destroyed.  I think I'm in an involuntary vacation. Not that I'm complaining," said Shaw.

"What's it like out there? Is it a media circus? The one time I'm involved in a big news worthy story and I'm left sleeping on a bed. Just my goddamn luck that I'd miss out on covering my own story."

"Hold on. It's not exactly like that, Jack. It's been a little quiet."

"You're not telling me that no one cares a giant Armadillo rampaged through the biggest proprietor of crickets as a food, are you?"

"It's not exactly that either."

"What about Ragazza, is she?"

"She didn't make it."

A knock came from the door. It was nurse Denham who walked in a moment later. She looked as good as ever. Her looks of course were always on point, but her complexion had returned. Her arm was open and no longer covered in sores.

"How are you feeling now Mr. Strafer?" she said.

"Fine, well rested," he said.

"That's good because for a while you were bogged down with the giggles. Some people thought you went mad, but I know Sunshower's special gorilla biscuits when I see them in effect," she said.

"Yeah well someone told me to calm down and I took their advice."

"You earned it. Shame that Sun couldn't have been here to hear what you were blathering about. Don't be worried, it was nothing too embarrassing, Mr. Strafer."

"I would have liked to have known him better. I would have liked to known any of them better."

"I know. It's hard to see anyone die especially the ways that Shaw explained. There will be time for mourning, but Mr. Strafer, there's someone here who needs to talk to you."

"Who is it?"

"It's a Mr. Lopes."

"I don't know a Mr. Lopes."

"I don't think you would considering he's from the FBI."

Jack looked at Shaw who nodded.

"Alright, sure," said Jack.

Shaw stood up and headed for the door.

"You're not staying?" said Jack.

"Don't worry, it's all standard procedure stuff," said Shaw.

A tall white man in a black suit came into the room. He was pale and wore a fedora. He looked Jack in the eye before sitting in Shaw's seat. He adjusted his tie and spoke with a calm direct voice.

"I'm special agent, Mr. Lopes. Jack Strafer, do you know what you did this morning?"

"I have an idea. I know my car and my arm are gone. I know I'm in a hospital filled with recovering lepers."

"You killed something from beyond our comprehension. You destroyed an invading force single-handedly."

"An invading force? It was one armadillo. Sure it was giant, but hardly an invasion."

"Yeah, a giant armadillo that could have ended life as we know it."

"You know something you're not telling me. What the hell was that thing? I'm guessing it wasn't just a giant mutated armadillo, was it?" said Jack.

"We may have known of such a creature before last night."

"Yeah I'm starting to figure that."

"We've already have our men examining the corpse. So far the autopsy is already proving our theory. We found bones inside its stomach suggesting that creature you killed had been here for a long time."

"What kind of bones?"

"Are you familiar with dinosaurs?"

"As much as anyone who loved them as a kid, sure," said Jack.

"There were bones found, a skull with three horns and a frill on it."

"You're telling me that you found a triceratops skull in the stomach of the Armordillo?"

"Along with the remains of the humans it ate, yes."

Jack's stomach churned and his face went white thinking about it.

"We also checked out the farms as per Mr. Shaw's suggestion. There was a fossil of a distressed Tyrannosaurus laying in the pit where we assume the Armordillo was nesting," said Lopes.

*A T. Rex fought this thing and lost? How the hell did I get so lucky?* Jack wiped his brow and the color returned to his face.

"Wait a minute. A triceratops and a T. Rex? How old was this thing? How was it even alive if was around eating dinosaurs?"

"We think it was in a deep sleep. A hibernation of sorts that allowed to survive for millions of years."

"Why would it wake up now?"

"It's possible the meteors woke it up. The vibrations through the Earth could be what triggered the monster to stir. It probably had enough of the shaking dirt and had decided to investigate what was disturbing its slumber."

"You mentioned a theory. What theory are you talking about?"

"We think the Armordillo originally came to Earth, 65 million years ago. We also don't think it was met with open arms from the dinosaurs. We don't know for sure, but it's possible that the Armordillo caused their extinction and the eternal winter that came with it.

"You said 'came to Earth,' You think it came from outer space?"

"Given that the Mars rover had found similar bones a few years ago. It's only natural to think this is a similar-"

"Wait, you mean on Mars? You're telling me that we found life on other planets and that the public doesn't know about it?"

"The public doesn't need to know that giant armadillos lived on Mars. We're not even sure they're originally from Mars. They might hop from planet to planet."

"How many of these things are you talking about?"

"The bones were found on Mars suggested the creature was pregnant. It seemed to be a litter of at least five. Those are the ones we found dead anyway. It's possible that they could have survived from one group or maybe they've spread out all over."

"What makes you think that?"

"We may have found similar bones on the moon and Ceres too."

"No one has ever been to Ceres."

"Not that you know."

"Fair enough. I figure there's all sorts of things we, the public, don't know."

"Mr. Strafer, I'll be straight with you. Either these creatures originated on Earth and were working their way out into the solar system or-"

"They were working their way to Earth."

"Exactly and we always knew it could appear at any moment if that were the case."

"Alright, I'm trying to wrap my head around all this; giant armadillo bones were found on all these dead planets and planetoids. Are you saying that this thing killed the solar system?"

"Not by itself, but its species may be responsible for the lack of life beyond Earth in out of our twelve planets."

"Eight planets,"

"Right, eight."

"I'm not going to go down that hole right now. I don't even understand why the hell you are telling me all of this."

"Because you're the first one to encounter this creature and you were able to destroy it."

"I'm sure your people or the military would have managed to kill it."

"Maybe yes, maybe no. We think that you killed it before it was fueled up. It was weak and you managed to finish it off before it regained full strength. If you didn't kill it then, who knows how powerful it may had become? It could have destroyed the entire planet. You saved the world. You're a hero to the country."

"It wasn't only me. I had some help, a lot actually."

"Unfortunately most of them are now dead. Their service will not be forgotten."

"And are you sure the Armordillo is dead? It didn't pop back up and start sludging people, did it?"

"We're sure Mr. Strafer. As I mentioned before we're already dissecting the bastard. We couldn't have found a dinosaur skull in its belly if it were still alive. You did a good job is what I'm saying Mr. Strafer. And to think this thing lost to a Ford Pinto."

"Thank you?"

"It's something to be proud of, but also we need to discuss some things."

"Like what?"

"Now you know you can't talk about this with anyone."

"Sure, but maybe I should be compensated for keeping my mouth shut?"

"Are you trying to blackmail the FBI?"

"No. You're the one giving me accolades for slaying a beast. I'm saying I should be awarded for killing a creature that could have cost millions in damages and death. It was my car and arm I lost after all. And you did just say that I saved the world."

The agent looked at Jack's missing arm.

"Fine," he scribbled into a pad, "Here's a check for 250,000. That should be enough for a new arm and a car. Don't get greedy, heroes are usually a little more humble."

"Not when they're on a journalist's salary."

The agent handed Jack the check and headed for the door.

"That's it?" said Jack.

"That's it, Mr. Strafer. Usually I'd talk a little more, but you cut to the chase for me."

"Hold on, what about all the people who already evacuated?"

"What about them?"

"Are they alright?"

"They're fine Mr. Strafer. We've stopped most of them on their way out of town and at the high school to administer a leprosy test."

"Then what?"

"If they have it, we'll help them."

"And if they don't?"

"Then they're free to go? What did you think we'd kill them or something?"

"How many people we infected?"

"None. Looks like this town got lucky thanks to you. It's a good thing you drove a forty year old piece of crap."

The agent left the room and Shaw replaced him. He stood at the foot of the bed.

"He sure does talk funny doesn't he?" said Shaw.

"Yeah a little sing-song vibe to him," said Jack.

"So what'd suit and tie Santa Claus give you?" said Shaw.

"Enough to keep my mouth shut."

"Mine too," said Shaw, "Looks like we made out okay."

"Yeah and we lost Ragazza, Sunshower, Rebecca-"

"We didn't lose Rebecca," said Shaw.

"What?"

"She's in the room next to yours. She's fine," said Shaw.

"Why didn't you tell me?"

"You've only been awake a few minutes and you didn't ask til now."

"Which room?"

"She's across the hall. Come on, get up, you're missing an arm, but your legs are fine," said Shaw.

Jack went across the hall and found Rebecca there laying in bed. She was watching TV with a smile on her face.

"Hey there Strafer," she said.

"Rebecca, you're alright?" he said.

"I need some rest, but yeah I'm fine," she said, "All the patients are. We nipped that leprosy like a gnat."

"Oh thank God," he said.

"Why are you worried about me anyway?"

"Cause I need to give something to my editor and we never finished our interview."

An hour later they sat at a table in Jim's bar. Shaw was picking at cricket fries and Rebecca was back to plopping dried crickets into her mouth like peanuts. Jack stared down at the burger beneath him. Three cold beers lay on the table with them. Jack asked Rebecca questions and he got them. Ones that weren't nearly as interesting as the ones he wished someone could answer. *Where did that monster come from? What did it want? Was it evil?* There was no one in the world who could satisfy those inquiries.

"Jack?" said Rebecca.

Jack looked at the dust on the walls and glanced at the patrons around him. Jim's bar had lost a few, but it didn't look like it made much of a difference. Jack had only been here at night, but he'd say business was doing much better since then. The place was packed full of people with all sorts of faces. There were young women, old men, anyone in between with hard and soft features. *What the hell were they doing here so early on a weekday? I guess since the factory's gone they're all unemployed. That must be it.*

"Jack!" said Rebecca.

Jack looked up.

"I thought I lost you there for a minute."

"No I'm good."

"Do you have any other questions for me?"

He looked at the notepad before it. It was the last piece of writing material he had. It was the last piece of himself he had. His car and materials within were destroyed. He saw the scribbles on the pad. There were notes, but he didn't remember jotting them down. He read over them and they seemed fine enough for a piece about the effects of meteors on crickets.

"I think that's it for questions," said Jack.

"What do you think you'll write next?" said Shaw.

"What do you mean? I'm writing about the crickets and the meteors," said Jack.

"I know that, but do you think you'll ever tell the real story?" said Shaw.

"I told the FBI I wouldn't."

"Yeah, but come on, the temptation has to be there," said Shaw.

"I'll admit, it is gnawing at me. I already came up with a perfect lead too," said Jack, "Hell I knew it came from space. I told you all it came from space."

"Yeah, a lucky guess you pulled out of your ass. My hat's off to you, Mr. Strafer. But what will you do now? If you're not going to write the Armordillo story that is," said Rebecca.

"I don't know. I guess go back home, find a new car, get a new arm," said Jack.

"Do you want to stick around and watch the meteors tonight?" said Shaw, "I think we earned the downtime."

"Yeah I actually know a great spot where we can see them fall all over Clapham," said Rebecca.

"I should check in with my editor," said Jack reaching into his pocket for his phone.

There were fifteen missed calls and thirty texts from his editor.

"Oh God, she's probably going to fire me for not answering," said Jack.

"Maybe she heard about the outbreak somehow and is worried?" said Rebecca.

"I'm going to step outside to call her," said Jack.

"Take your time," said Shaw.

Rebecca plopped more crickets into her mouth and Shaw sipped at a beer. More cars were pulling into the parking lot. Jack had only been here a short while, but it really did seemed packed. The day was already sinking away as Jack rang up his editor. She answered on the second ring.

"Hey Susan."

"God damn Jack it's about time. I been trying to get a hold of you all day."

"Look, I'm sorry. It's been a crazy night and day. My car exploded and I've been in the hospital."

"I know. You were sending me pics and texts from the ambulance. And then some more from the hospital bed."

"What sort of pics and texts?"

"Of the Armordillo, stupid. It's some of the best writing you ever did," she said.

"Jesus, I did?"

"Yeah, it's some really great camera work too. That doctor knew how to frame a shot. You weren't bad either," she said.

"Susan you need to delete everything I sent you,"

"What are you nuts? This is great," she said.

"We can't publish any of it. I already told the FBI I wouldn't."

"You must have been really high this morning, weren't you?"

"What's that have to do with anything? I may have been-"

"I don't care if you were high or get high every night, Jack. It's a little too late for you to tell the FBI no considering you already made it live on the website this morning."

"Maybe I can take it down," he said.

"Jack I don't think you understand, major news outlets are already picking up the story."

"Oh God."

"What are you upset about Jack? This story has brought more traffic to our site than any other story in five years. This is it Jack, this is the big-time. Everyone wants to interview you, me, anyone who has anything to do with the Armordillo."

"Yeah and what about the goddamn FBI? They're going to have me arrested or killed or charged with treason," said Jack.

"Screw those alphabet suits. We have lawyers for this type of thing. This story is going to put us on top. You won't be stuck covering kid's sports no more. We can finally get back to real reporting Jack."

"I've got to say, I wouldn't mind covering a game or two after last night," said Jack.

"Really? There is soccer season starting next week, but I thought you'd rather cover the political race instead. One candidate was said to have killed her husband and framed his brother. But if you want to keep covering kids sports, that's fine by me Jack. It's your pick," she said.

"I'll take the politics," said Jack.

"You got it Jack, that'll be your assignment when you get back," she said.

"When am I expected back? I'm a little lacking in the transportation department at the moment."

"You'll probably be done fielding questions there in about a week," she said.

"Wait, hold on. What, you mean here in Clapham? You want me to stay?"

"Of course. You're our man in the field. Think of it as a little paid time off."

"What about the meteor story?"

"I'm still expecting that at the end of the week," she said.

"You did good Jack. You did real good," she said.

"Thanks," he said.

Susan hung up on him and Jack slipped the phone back away. Jack walked back inside Jim's bar. An attractive young woman walked up to him.

"Are you Jack Strafer?" she said.

"Yeah that'd be me," he said.

"It's a pleasure to meet you," she said extending a hand towards Jack's missing one.

She paused and her eyes grew wide.

"Oh my God, did you lose your arm to the Armordillo? That's so brave," she said.

"No, that's been like that for awhile," he said laughing.

"I'm with the KWY News network. Do you mind if I ask you a few questions?" she said.

"Is it about the Armordillo?"

"What else would it be about?" she said.

"I'm actually with my friends right now," he said.

"It'll only take a few minutes," she said.

"Maybe later," he said.

Jack walked away to sit back down with Rebecca and Shaw. He took a bite of the cricket burger and didn't even wince when swallowing it.

A short man with thick rimmed glasses approached them at the table.

"Are you Jack Strafer?" he said.

"Yes," said Jack looking at Rebecca and Shaw.

"And you two must be Shaw and Rebecca," he said.

They nodded.

"What do you want?" said Jack.

"I'm with the MGH News Network. I'm here to do a piece on you," he said.

"Can it wait? I'm in the middle of eating here," said Jack.

"I don't like making my readers wait Mr. Strafer. It'll only take ten minutes of your time," he said.

"Sure ten minutes from you then another ten minutes from every two bit reporter who's showing up here," said Jack.

The man in glasses sat down at the table.

"Make it quick," said Jack.

Another three reporters lined up to ask them the same questions. None of which were anything not covered by the initial article written by Jack. The typical fluff questions to provide clickbait to their websites. *Was it scary? How did you find the courage? Do you believe what happened?*

They eventually made their escape. They found themselves on a bill hill overlooking Clapham. Shaw brought out some lawn chairs from Rebecca's SUV and the three of them sat and watched.

They could see the headlights pulling into town. Soon there'd be hundreds here to see where the giant monster attacked. That wasn't what they came to see.

It was a crystal clear night. The stars were shining and the show was about to start.

The meteors weren't invited but they fell all the same. They landed all over the farms of Clapham, Texas. At least thirty had survived the atmosphere. They laid in craters. Slowly they began to uncurl. Little heads poked out and long armored noses sniffed the air.

## About

Michael Polillo holds a bachelor's in journalism from Rowan University. He lives in southern New Jersey and grew up on a steady diet of kaiju movies, spaghetti westerns, and pulp books. Now he writes horror, dark comedies, and science fiction.

Subscribe to my mailing list to stay up to date on my latest release http://eepurl.com/gRQ4Qn

Follow me on Twitter @MikePolillo and Instagram @countpupper

## Other Titles

I'm Sal: The Soft Boiled Mobster – A crime thriller with mobster Sal Corbucci about his journey to find a missing daughter of a retired boxer.

The Girl with the Electric Eye – A sci-fi western with bounty hunter Ashley Morris searching for the woman who took her eye.

We're Bitches – A horror about three men stuck in a beach house full of lady werewolves looking to make them their next meal.

All titles available in paperback and ebook.